# Shenkin's Legacy

*Davey Davies*

Clink Street

Published by Clink Street Publishing 2024

Copyright © 2024

First edition.

ISBN:
978-1-915785-57-2 - paperback
978-1-915785-58-9 - ebook

## Also by Davey Davies

Shenkin

Shenkin's Vengeance

# Acknowledgments

Victorian Era Women's Rights    VL McBeath

The Duelling Handbook    Joseph Hamilton

Steam at Sea    Denis Griffiths

Victorian Style    Judith & Martin Miller
The Ball in the novels of    Jane Austen

Rock Davis Shipyard    Wikipedia Article

The Ball inspired by the novels of    Jane Austen

My continued appreciation to my good friend John William Foster
for his assistance, and above all, his patience.

To family and friends for their support and understanding while the author
locked himself in his study, while writing about his other family: the Shenkins.

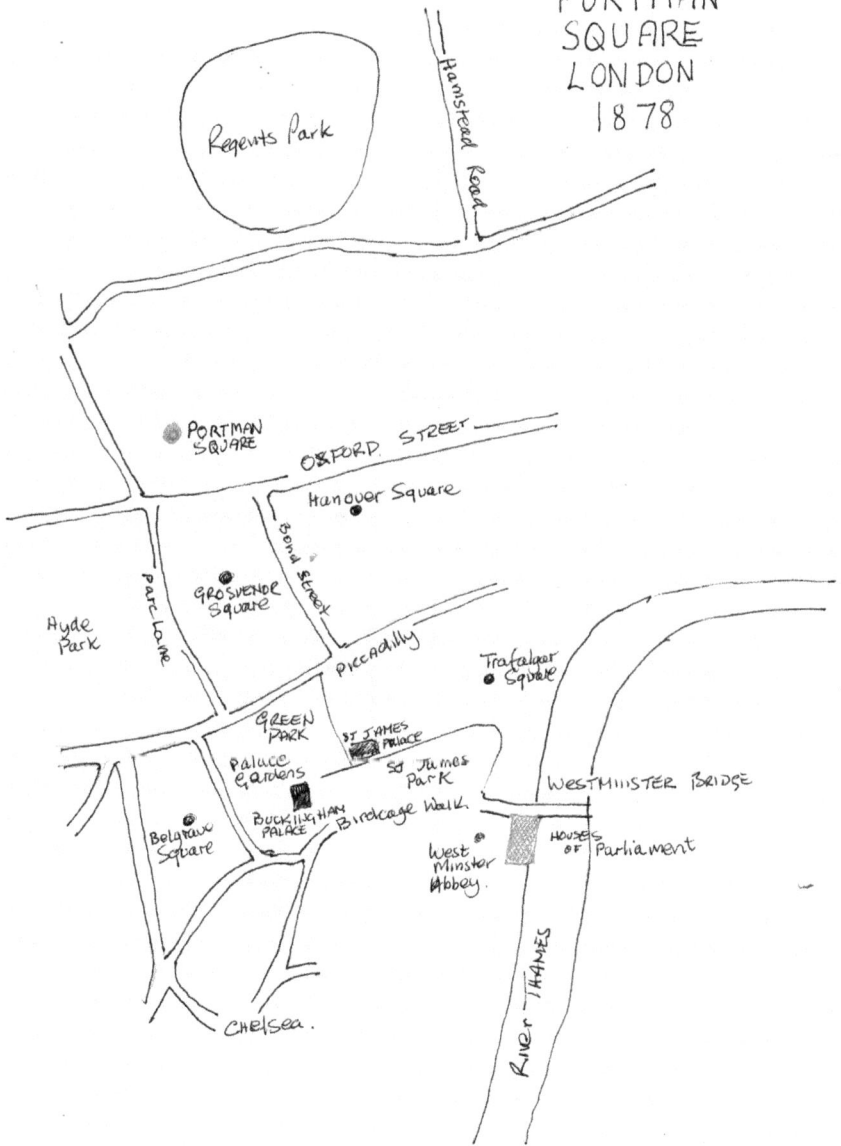

PORTMAN SQUARE LONDON 1878

Regents Park

Hamstead Road

PORTMAN SQUARE

OXFORD STREET

Hanover Square

Bond Street

GROSVENOR Square

Hyde Park

Park Lane

Piccadilly

Trafalgar Square

GREEN PARK

ST JAMES PALACE

St James Park

WESTMINSTER BRIDGE

Palace Gardens

Belgrave Square

BUCKINGHAM PALACE

Birdcage Walk

West Minster Abbey

HOUSES OF Parliament

Chelsea.

RIVER THAMES

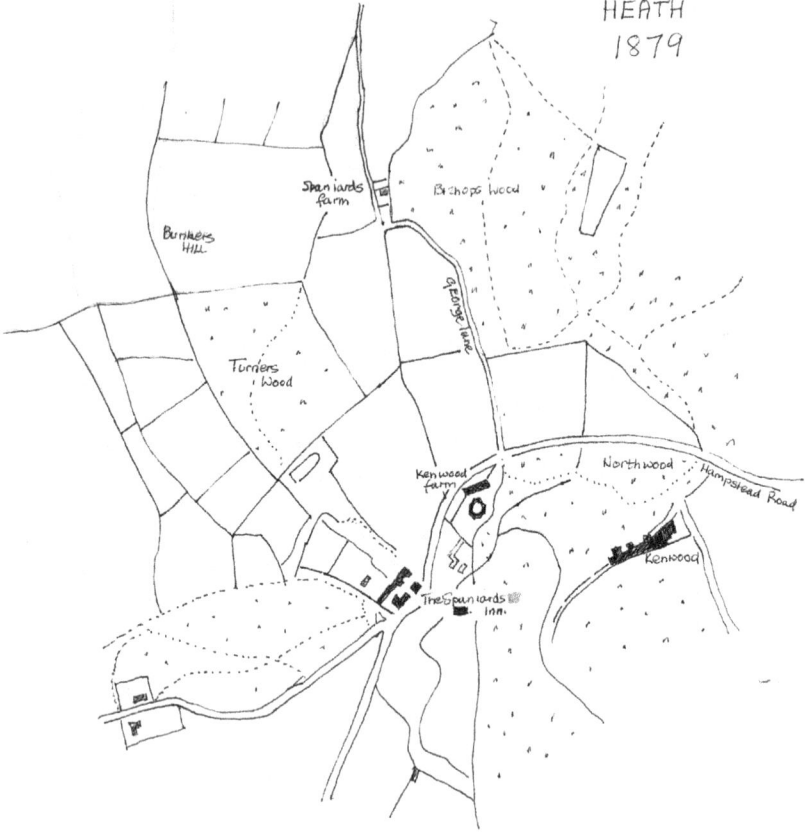

SITE OF DUEL
HAMPSTEAD
HEATH
1879

Spaniards
farm

Bishops Wood

Bunkers
Hill

George Lane

Turners
Wood

Kenwood
farm

Northwood

Hampstead Road

Kenwood

The Spaniards
Inn

*To Allanah Margaret Davies*

*First God created man, and then
he had a much better idea*

*The things you do for yourself are gone when you are gone, but the things you do for others remain as your legacy*

KALU NDUKWE KALU

# PREFACE

Following many readers' responses to the first two books, *Shenkin* and *Shenkin's Vengeance*, I had a number of emails asking when the third book in the series was to be published.

While all the books stand alone as a story line in themselves, the third book, *Shenkin's Legacy*, completes a trilogy dealing with the same characters. After spending a number of years writing about Daniel Shenkin, his courage and determination to survive against the odds in the mines of South Wales and the brutality of the convict ships, while being transported to the penal colonies of Australia and Tasmania with a twenty-year hard-labour sentence for leading a rising against the sovereign state to improve the working conditions of ordinary working men, I feel the loss of a close friend.

We burned the midnight oil together while I wrote about his struggles, his bare-knuckle fighting, his escape from the notorious penal settlement at Port Arthur and his success as a sheep station owner, which made him a wealthy man. And his long bitter fight with the House of Feltsham. Lord Percival Hugo Feltsham caused the death of the woman he loved and that of his two closest friends. He finally saw the downfall of Lord Percival, and in the years that followed, Daniel Shenkin became a very rich successful businessman.

His daughter Beth Shenkin married Daniel's oldest friend Sir Edward Standish's son, Sir Justin Standish, and moved to London. Shenkin, now in ill health, is determined to go back to his coal-black Welsh valley with his cut man from his bare-knuckle fighting days, the Aborigine Tinker.

Beth travels down from London to visit her father, but the news is not good.

Now I'll let you read what happens. It's not all red roses and warm embraces, but I hope you will enjoy it and perhaps you too will burn the midnight oil reading about the Shenkin family. For those who wrote to me from Australia, America and the UK, thank you, also for a number of good book write-ups, which were greatly appreciated. I trust it meets with all your expectations.

# CHAPTER 1

The wind gusted hard on the dark mountainside, while the rain came down in driving sheets of icy cold blasts. Both elements battered hard against the six-sided coffin as the pallbearers swayed in their long slow walk towards the open grave. Gravediggers, ropes at the ready, stood waiting to cradle the coffin on its final journey.

As the coffin hung for a moment in the air, the wind caught the side of it. The pallbearers fought to cradle it onto the ropes, but the front of the coffin hit the muddy earth with a loud thud. Nervously, the mourners watched while the coffin was righted and lowered slowly into the ground.

Beth Shenkin stood by the side of her father's grave weeping. The cold rain mixed with her warm tears as she bent her head in sorrow. All was wet and windy in the old cemetery above the dark-clouded, coal-covered town of Merthyr Tydfil in South Wales. Once the coffin was laid to rest, each mourner scattered wet coal-black clay earth onto the coffin lid that bore a single brass plaque *Daniel Shenkin 1810 – 1878 'So it shall be'*.

After some time, when the gravediggers and pallbearers were paid and only the mourners and the chapel pastor remained, Beth raised her head to the wind. The pastor watched but remained silent, for Shenkin wanted no prayers spoken over him. Shenkin believed in mankind, not in a man made god. He and the pastor had had many arguments over this since Shenkin had returned to his black valley. After his last heart attack, the doctors in Sydney and London had given him perhaps two years to live, if he took care. Tinker, his close Aboriginal friend, made sure that he did. That it was five years before the heart finally called the last round bore witness to Tinker's care.

The pastor, Mr Thomas Thomas, known to his parishioners as Thomas the Chapel, would miss their talks which, while heated, were always respectful of each other's beliefs. He slowly walked over to Beth. 'A sad moment, my dear, my deepest condolences.'

'Thank you, Mr Thomas. He spoke of you many times.'

Thomas the Chapel gave a small smile. 'Probably through gritted teeth.'

'His very expression,' Beth said.

They both gave a small nervous laugh.

'You'll be returning to London, then?'

'Yes, but first I'll be starting the arrangements for turning the big house into a foundation centre for the poor and needy.'

'He spoke of it to me over these too short years that I knew him; it's a fine generous thing to do. If there is anything I can do, please let me know, Lady Standish.'

'Thank you and it's Beth please. We'll also be opening one in London and another in Sydney. The Shenkin Charity Foundation Centres will be his legacy. They'll be dedicated to helping the poor and needy of this troubled world, a sanctuary of protection for the homeless.'

'I'll pray for their success, Beth.'

Finally, the moment was broken. The wind blew hard as the sharp rain began turning to sleet. They gave their last glances at the muddy-topped coffin that held the body of a once-warm-hearted man, now in the cold black earth of his homeland.

Tinker turned.

'We need to go, Beth,' said the white-haired, black-faced Aboriginal man standing on the gravelled path between the lines of graves, his lips blue with the cold, his eyes filled with silent tears. His Aboriginal name was Tallara Warron-Wurrah, he possessed a strong but quiet dignity, and Shenkin had named him Tinker for ease of pronunciation many years ago.

'In a moment, Tinker, in a moment.' The elegant man at Tinker's side lifted his bowed head.

'Tinker's right, Beth, let's get back to the house and out of this rain before we all catch pneumonia.' The man was Sir Justin Standish, Beth's husband, the member of parliament for Surrey, her love, closest friend and support.

'Yes, you're both right, my dears.'

Looking down at the muddy cold earth, she said, 'Well, Shenkin, I can tell you one thing, it will not end here. Your legacy will continue. I'll make sure of that; I promise you.'

Then, turning slowly, she walked over to Justin and Tinker.

'Let's go my dears. Regrettably, there's nothing more we can do here.'

'No, for death is as natural as life, a beginning and an end. It is the same for all things,' said Tinker. There was a catch in the old man's voice as cold and as icy as the morning wind. A wind that was now full of white swirling flakes of snow in contrast to the black coal dust that covered the valley. It blew into the grave, placing a light apron of white over the coffin.

Taking a deep breath, Beth said, 'We'll close the house up, then travel to London. Do you want to return to Sydney and the warm, Tinker?'

'No, my place is with you. He made me promise that.'

'But...'

'There are no buts, Beth, if Shenkin said so, so it will be,' Tinker said, tight sobs still separating his words.

'How many times have I heard that over the years?'

'He never failed to fulfil the promise.'

'No never. Dear God, I'll miss him so much, Tinker.'

Tinker nodded. Justin squeezed her hand.

'I'm alright, my dear. It just seems so very, very final. But the children must be seen to and cared for, and you must get back to your duties in parliament and life must go on,' said Beth, in a positive strong voice.

She was a tall handsome woman. Even now in her early thirties men turned to take in her beauty. She had already lived a life fuller than most do in many lifetimes. Wet to the skin and chilled to her bones, she mentally pledged herself to Shenkin's legacy.

# CHAPTER 2

After a few weeks of discussions with the lawyers, regarding converting the big house where Shenkin's mother once scrubbed the floors into the first Shenkin Foundation Centre for the poor, Beth finally prepared to leave for their London home and the children.

On the long journey by private carriage back to London, Beth went over the events in her life. Born in Sydney, Australia, her mother Elizabeth had died soon after her birth. Her biological father was a convict serving a twenty-year sentence for crimes against the state. He was sent to the notorious Port Arthur Penal Prison on Van Diemen's Land, while she found herself with Lord Percival Hugo Feltsham, who had coveted her mother, Elizabeth Moxey. He had married Elizabeth on her deathbed to gain her dowry, leaving her daughter Beth at his mercy. He was a debauched stepfather who had no time for a child in his life.

Beth would be locked in her room, sometimes for days at a time, while her stepfather gambled with his cronies, and his second wife, a dedicated social climber, entertained her influential friends. Neither were remotely interested in the child in their care, nor was her nanny, who was more of a jailer than any kind of companion. She had no governess to guide her in her letters, so she had no education. A grim sad look spread across Beth's handsome face as the rattler bounced and pitched on the carriage-rutted roads. It all came flooding back to her: the beatings, the humiliations, the abusive behaviour.

Her mind wandered. She remembered a party dress she liked and had wanted to wear one evening, it was festooned with cornflower-coloured blue ribbons, the colour of her eyes. A friend of her so-called stepmother had given it to her for her birthday. It had been her daughter's dress, but she had outgrown it.

'Please let me wear it tonight, sir.'

Feltsham insisted she call him sir.

'No, we do not wear hand-me-down clothes.' He then rang for a servant.

After a moment, his manservant, a former convict, came to the door of the study. 'You rang sir?'

'Stoke the fire up to a good blaze.'

'Very well sir.'

Beth turned to leave, tears rolling down her cheeks. 'Stay, child,' said Feltsham, in a harsh tone.

The fire now danced in fierce flames, wood crackled into submission.

Feltsham beckoned the servant to him. 'Take the dress this child is holding and put it on the fire.'

'My lord, I don't understand. You mean for me to burn the dress?'

'Are you questioning me?'

'No sir but...'

'Get on with it, you imbecile, or I'll have you back in chains again.'

The servant, with a look of sorrow in his eyes, walked over to Beth.

'Sorry miss,' he whispered.

The bright blue ribbons caught alight first. Beth sobbed at the sight.

'Be quiet child, or you go to bed without any supper,' said Feltsham, his voice slurred with drink. Adding, 'Do you hear?'

'Yes sir, I hear and I'll never forgive you. Do you hear that?'

Feltsham, his face red with anger, moved quickly across the room and struck Beth across the face.

The servant, a big powerful man, caught Feltsham's arm as he went to strike Beth again.

'Enough sir, she's only a child.'

Feltsham glared at him, walked over to his writing desk, opened a draw, took out a loaded pistol, raised it and shot the man in the head.

Blood spurted from the open wound onto Beth. She screamed.

Soon the room was full of the other house servants, together with Feltsham's wife.

Lady Feltsham, a fan in one hand and a powder puff in the other, demanded to know what was happening.

'Send for the police constables from Sydney my dear. Speak to Chief Constable Browning; tell him it's urgent.'

'What shall I say?'

'That I have been attacked by an ex-convict in my own home.'

'No, that's not....' Beth started to say, but Feltsham cut her short.

'The child's hysterical. Clean her up and take her to her room,' Feltsham said. Then, turning to the tight-lipped, sharp-nosed nanny at Beth's side, he added, 'She is to stay there until I say otherwise.'

The nanny bowed her head. 'Very good sir,' she said, pulling Beth to her roughly.

Later that evening, the chief constable, a rather stout man, sat comfortably, if overflowing, in a highly decorated Thomas Hope settee, a glass of Glenlivet placed at his side on a handsome leather-topped desk, while Feltsham offered him a box of his finest cigars.

Raising his glass, Feltsham said, in his most charming of manners, 'To George Smith's Scottish Distillery, my dear Browning, for his excellent smooth whisky.'

Smooth indeed, for Browning believed every word of Lord Feltsham's explanation. He commiserated with his lordship for the ordeal he had been through. The body was removed, the blood cleaned up, and all was forgotten in a cloud of Figurado smoke.

This was but one of many such episodes that Beth was subjected to. By the time she was nine years old, his drunken abusive behaviour became terrifying. Beatings for the smallest of mistakes, and worse still, sexual advances that left Beth in a state of constant fear. Too frightened to sleep, she would hide in the many rooms of the big house, or the outside gardens, searching for a safe place.

Her stepmother or nanny offered no security or comfort to her. They simply did not care. Finally, when she was eleven, almost twelve years old, a man came to see Feltsham. He was a tall elegant man. She observed him while cowering from behind a heavy curtain that led to Feltsham's study. Raised voices came from the room. Beth did not know the circumstances, but the man was Sir Edward Standish, whose refined voice spoke in measured tones to Feltsham.

'Those are the terms you agreed on when you last spoke to Daniel Shenkin. So you will send for the child and her nanny immediately Lord Feltsham, and hand them over to me.' An aristocrat to his fingertips, Sir Edward sat and waited while Feltsham continued to rant and rave. Then, grasping the bell cord, he too sat down, brushed lint from his coat cuff and turned to Sir Edward.

'Shenkin is welcome to the brat. I'm glad to see her go,' he said, while still searching for the illusive piece of lint on his sleeve.

A servant came to the door. 'You rang sir?'

'Send for the child and the nanny, and be quick about it.'

'Very good sir.'

Moments later, Beth stood in the doorway of the study, her clothes in disarray, her hair uncombed while she struggled to break free from the grip of the nanny.

'You wanted to see us sir?'

'Get the brat's clothes packed. You are both to go with this man.'

'But I'm employed here sir, am I not?'

'There is no child here woman, so I no longer need a nanny.'

17

'But…'

'Just do it, you stupid woman, just do it! This gentleman will either require your services or not, in which case you will go back to the female convict prison in the rocks, where you belong. So get on with it.'

By now, both Beth and the nanny were sobbing as they made their way up to Beth's room.

'Listen to the screeching and wailing,' Feltsham said. 'Shenkin's welcome to them, and what about the cost of their upkeep these past ten or so years?'

'You've agreed terms with Shenkin, Feltsham. I wouldn't push it further if I were you.'

'Take the bitches. My wife's also gone, so I'll be saved from their continual complaints and female chatter.'

'A lonely life sir, a very lonely life, which I feel you richly deserve.'

'Go before I set the house dog on you.'

Removing a Derringer from his inside pocket, Standish said, 'I wouldn't recommend it your lordship, unless, of course, you want to lose a fine dog too.'

An hour later, they were in a coach on their way to Bare Knuckle Sheep Station and her father, to be reunited after so many lost years.

Shenkin had much to explain to Beth, but first he dismissed the nanny from her station and the house. Then he turned to his assembled friends. 'Gentlemen, may I introduce you to my daughter, Beth.' Strange that such a strong face should hold a tear in each eye, even stranger that Beth should notice it, but she did. It caused her to stop crying.

In the days and months that followed, Beth spent many hours talking to Shenkin, who slowly and carefully went over the past with her. His meeting with her mother Elizabeth on the convict ship the *Runnymede*. Her mother's death, caused by Lord Feltsham at the hands of his henchman Ketch.

It was difficult for a child to comprehend it all, but the truth was planted in her mind and she nurtured it as best she could. Certainly her life had changed from one of cruelty to one of love, kindness and gentle consideration for her wellbeing. All of Shenkin's friends gave their side of the story. An old photograph taken in London, by a process only just being developed in Europe, of her uncle, Captain Josiah Moxey, and his niece, her mother Elizabeth Moxey, about to board the convict ship the *Runnymede*.

Sir Edward Standish walked with her around the pastures of BKSS. 'I know my dear, it's hard to take it all in but give it time. You certainly have his temper and determination and your mother's beauty. He loved your mother so much, as he now loves you; it's driven him to this moment.'

Tinker the aborigine, who was Shenkin's shadow, taught her about herbs, flowers and plants, and that his god was all around them in the earth, mountains and sky.

And so the months passed and then the years. Happy years with her father, who spoke to her often about her mother Elizabeth and his love for her.

The carriage stopped to change horses, waking Beth from her memories. 'A light meal in the tavern my dear, and then back to the coach,' Justin said.

# CHAPTER 3

The carriage bumped and rolled while the late spring countryside moved jerkily past the windows. Justin Standish leaned forward. 'Are you alright, my dear? Perhaps we should have taken one of the new horse-drawn trams the railways are developing?'

'I'm alright Justin, don't fret. I'm just going over the past in my mind. We'll soon see the children and that will brighten us up, will it not?'

'Indeed it will. Tinker's fast asleep, poor chap. It's all too much for him now.'

'He should return to Australia to the warm, but having given his word to Shenkin to stay with me then he won't, of course,' Beth said, with a sigh.

'No,' said Justin. 'What Shenkin said was, and still is, the law. My father always says the same. Daniel Shenkin had that effect upon people. I wonder how my father is faring in Sydney? The family want to return to London, but he's determined to hold on to his independence for as long as possible.' Then with a sigh, he said, 'There's not many of the old crowd still left and the mail takes so long to get to each other, even with the three-pence "Sydney View" stamps on them. The view depicts a female to represent industry directing the attention of newly arrived convicts to the virtues of honest work in the form of oxen-ploughing free labour. It's outrageous,' Justin said, shaking his head in dismay.

'Raise the question in parliament, my dear.'

'The Palace of Westminster is at the moment more interested in trying to change the two-house system. The House of Lords block so many of our bills, my dear, and by men who are not even elected. Which reminds me, I understand that one of Lord Feltsham's family, a first cousin, or nephew I understand, is Lord Algernon Hugo Feltsham, who now sits in the Lords. It's a hereditary title so he's entitled to do so, by virtue of the fact that he's a lineal descendant of the original peer.'

'Why should this be of interest to me Justin? The Feltsham business is long over; he got his just deserts and that's an end of it,' Beth said.

Justin gave a sigh. 'He may prove to be a problem, my dear. I did not wish to bring it up sooner, given Shenkin's passing and the funeral, but he's spreading rumours around the House of Lords regarding his stolen inheritance. That his uncle Lord Percival was cheated out of his holdings in Australia, which included opal mines, sheep stations, ships and bank assets together with his good name. Stolen by one Daniel Shenkin, an escaped convict.' Justin placed his hand on hers. 'Now keep calm Beth.'

Beth stood up in the swaying carriage and fell into the vernacular of her native tongue. 'The bloody man has no right to say such things. I'll sue the bastard for slander.'

Tinker woke up with a start. 'Are we home?'

# CHAPTER 4

'A fortune sir,' Lord Algernon Hugo Feltsham said, sipping his after-dinner brandy. Adding, 'An absolute fortune.'

Taking a deep breath, he continued, 'Sheep stations, opal mines, shipping and properties, don't you know? A considerable amount of wealth, all stolen from him by this convict. A man who had even assumed another man's name and, as such, acquired that man's property too.' His voice boomed across the dining room of his club at Boodle's in St James's Street.

Ash fell from the cigar of the man he was speaking to. 'What do you intend to do about it, my dear chap?' Adding, 'But please keep your voice down, my lord.'

'Do! Do about it? Why, come the recess, I intend to go to Sydney and expose the man as a cheat, a swindler and an impostor sir, that's what,' he said in an unchanged vocal tone. 'But firstly, I will charge his surviving daughter with coming to England under false colours.'

'The man's dead then,' said the older man. 'Most difficult, sir. I speak now as both your friend and your lawyer. However, you say his daughter lives here in England?'

'Indeed so, here in London, in fact, the wife of Sir Justin Standish, the MP for Surrey.'

'Where?'

'Portman Square, a mere stone's throw from here. And on my rightful money too. Why the Standishes allowed their son to marry a convict's daughter is beyond me and a social scandal.'

'It gets better; she may well want to avoid the scandal, but this all happened in New South Wales. Is that not so?'

'Which is why I intend to go there, sir.'

'A long way to go, my dear fellow, a very long way.'

Lord Algernon shrugged his shoulders. 'But a fortune sits there and it's mine. Whatever it takes, I intend to claim it.'

'It will come down to a question of reputation and creditability, sir and if I remember rightly, if you forgive me for saying, your uncle had creditors at his heels when he left London for Australia, leaving his mother to face his creditors and she ending up in Marshalsea Street Debtors Prison did she not?'

Lord Algernon Hugo Feltsham bristled with indignation. Red in the face, he turned to his dining companion. 'Are you accusing a member of my family of disreputable behaviour sir?' Adding, 'I assure you it was all an unfortunate misunderstanding.'

Knowing the temper Lord Algernon possessed, his friend nodded. 'Of course, my dear chap, of course. Let's say no more about it. Now, how and when do you intend to leave?'

'Within two to three months, across the summer recess. I'll ask for leave of absence from attending the House of Lords. They have their quota of life peers and hereditary peers, together with the usual twenty-six bishops. So there should be no problem. I'll ask for special dispensation not to be called to vote, if the need arises, on the grounds of pressing family business that may well take a number of months. Until then, we have the social whirl to deal with, which reminds me, are you attending the Hastings' ball?'

'Indeed I am sir. It's the food, you know; I never miss it,' the older man said, giving cause for further cigar ash to cascade down the front of his black frock tailed coat. He was beginning to look like a speckled tortoise.

Lord Algernon bowed slightly. 'Till then, my dear chap, when I hope to have my plans laid.'

Justin looked up as Beth entered the drawing room. In his hand he held a card from off the Adam fireplace.

'The invitation to Lady Hastings' bash is this weekend, I see. It will take your mind off of Lord Feltsham, will it not?'

Beth moved to his side. 'The bloody man now has his sister Lady Cordelia spreading rumours about Shenkin. It's just not acceptable, and there's talk that he intends to go to Sydney during the summer recess of the House of Lords. Have you heard anything in Westminster?'

'Yes, gossip is doing the rounds, I regret to say.'

Beth shook her head in dismay. 'Well, it's already causing some questions to be asked.'

'How so?'

'The purchase of the London house for Shenkin's Foundation Centre off Berkeley Square has been withdrawn this afternoon. It's where I've just come from. They refuse to give a reason, but let slip that certain rumours had come to their attention; they would say no more. The bloody, bloody people, I'll not stand for it,' Beth said, standing upright with tight fists.

'No, of course, it's scandalous, but difficult to contain. The Feltsham family do still have the ear of society. Let us leave it for this evening my dear; we'll go to the ball and meet friends there. It will take your mind off of it. What do you say?'

# CHAPTER 5

It had taken her father, Daniel Shenkin, an escape from Port Arthur Penal Colony and then long difficult years to get his daughter back. When he did, she was almost twelve years old – scared, but feisty. She had been the victim of the drunken advances of Feltsham, the hatred of his lordship's wife and the disinterested care of an ex-convict nanny. Not the best start to a young life.

When a few days later they had finally arrived back home to Portman Square, she had walked up to the front door, which suddenly burst open to let loose two excited little children.

'Mummy, Daddy,' came a chorus of shrieking voices, closely followed by their plump nanny, all fluster and smiles. 'Sorry my lady, I just couldn't stop them. They've been so excited all day.'

'It's alright Molly. I understand,' Beth said, holding them both to her tightly.

'What did you bring us, Mummy?' Effie, their daughter, wanted to know.

'Did you bring us a whale that can swim?' said Edward

'Wales is a country Edward, not a fish,' Sir Justin said sternly, and then smiled. 'Anyway, we couldn't get it into the coach, could we, Mother?'

They all went into the house, laughter and all. They were greeted by the rest of the household servants.

'We did eat on the way, but rather a long time back Mrs Lawson, so we're looking forward to your home cooking.' And turning to the children, Beth said, 'You'll find some parcels in the coach marked with your names. Molly, would you take them and the presents up to their rooms please?'

'I will so, Beth.'

After the excitement of being back in London, Beth was slowly coming to terms with the rumours that the Feltsham family were spreading about Shenkin.

'Yes, perhaps a weekend at the Hastings' will be good for us; June and July sees the place at its best. Hopefully the rumours have not reached Florence's ears yet. But she knows all about my background and was always supportive in our friendship.'

'You were at finishing school with her, of course.'

'Indeed, a tough rough Australian girl straight from a smelly sheep station on the other side of the world. A ragamuffin with few social graces, no dress sense, and a broad accent you could cut timber with. Placed in a posh school for young ladies. They made fun of me, teased me about my speech and the way I walked and ate. Then I met seventeen-year-old Lady Wells, as she was then, the school's head girl. Shenkin had made a donation to the Geneva school, hence my acceptance, and Florence made a speech thanking him for his generosity. I presented her with the cheque that your father had given me three months before in Sydney.' Beth smiled a slow smile and sighed.

'We became friends immediately. She never criticised my shortcomings or laughed at my lack of social graces but, instead, she gently advised me on what to do, what to wear, the right knife and fork to use and not to speak with my mouth full.' At this, they both laughed.

'She stood up for me against the other girls' jibes and ridicule. I never had any further problems. During the holidays, since I had so far to go home, she invited me to meet her parents, who greeted me with open arms. We became such close friends.'

Justin gave a smile. 'I remember meeting her for the first time at our wedding and being impressed with her uncritical view of our marriage, given the petty uproar it caused among the more snobbish attitude of some society ladies.'

After a moment Beth said, 'She is the only true lady I have ever met; it will be good to see her again.'

Their journey to the Hastings' seat in Tunbridge Wells was pleasant and Beth felt more relaxed to be leaving the rumours behind them, if only for a short while.

It was almost dark by the time they arrived; the arrangement was to stay overnight and so be fresh for the next evening's ball. The long ride along the drive to the house set the scene for the Hastings' beautiful grand house. A pile of wonderfully proportioned stone that made a statement of wealth and power that reached back to the Hundred Years War when Edward of Woodstock, the Black Prince, bestowed lands and position on the first Lord Hastings at the battle of Poitiers in 1356. On the paved entrance stood Lady Florence, her arms wide open, while two hunting dogs sat obediently at her side and her children, Emily and William, stood in front of her. They were surrounded by a bevy of servants who were coming and going at silent speed. Luggage and hat boxes were removed from their carriage and swiftly taken to their appointed rooms. Stable hands were leading the horses away to be rubbed down, watered and fed.

'Florrie!' Beth called, opening her arms wide.

The two women stood for a while in each other's arms. 'Pregnancy suits you, Florrie. How long to go?' said Beth, kissing the children.

'Another month yet, but it's going according to nature, so all is fine. It's just difficult to move around and I fear falling over either the dogs or the children.'

'We'll watch out for you, won't we, Justin?'

Justin bent forward and kissed her on her cheek, a bouquet of dried flowers in his hands.

'For a beautiful woman who is soon to be an even more beautiful mother.'

'Flattery and charm, you must come more often,' Florence said, with a laugh. 'I'll make two garlands for us to wear to tomorrow night, Beth?' She smiled a warm smile. 'Just as if we were sisters, my dear.' Which she felt in mind and soul they were. 'I'm so very pleased that you are here.' Florence said, holding Beth to her again.

Then turning, Florence said, 'Jason, Rex, heel.' The two dogs sprung to their feet and padded beside her into the main hall; the children ran ahead. It was as Beth remembered it, cavernous with a line of glittering chandeliers hung from the ceiling for the whole length of the hall in a statement of elegance and grace. Beth preferred their other beautiful name, 'ceiling roses', fragile, delicate, but strong and regal, festooned with strings of glittering glass and crystal drops. Beth remembered Florrie had told her that James's great grandfather Lord Nathaniel Hastings had purchased them in Venice in the late 17th century. They had adorned the hall ever since.

'Stop staring upwards, Beth, and follow me to your rooms.'

Beth laughed. 'Those shining orbs of glass and gold are so very beautiful, don't you think so, Justin?'

'I do my dear. They take one's breath away,' he said, as they began to climb the grand staircase. At the top of the first flight facing them was a painting of James's late father in the colourful robes of the high sheriff of the county. From here, stairs led off right and left to the east and west wings.

'I've put you in the west wing, Beth, knowing how much you like to look out onto the gardens.'

'Wonderful, Florrie. Thank you.'

The Vista room was lavishly decorated with silk-covered, ornate French-style furniture, which surrounded a large four-poster bed. A maid stood ready to unpack their trunk. The trunk had been given to them as a wedding gift by Shenkin's dear friend Captain John Saxon. It was a sea captain's uniform travel case in English leather with brass clasps and carrying handles at each side. Inside lay Beth's two Rococo ball gowns and Justin's dinner jackets side by side, ready for their wardrobe hangers. The compartments of accessories were soon placed on the dressing table: all Beth's perfumes of rose, violets and bergamot, together with skin creams and handkerchiefs to carry the scents. Beth's Eau de Cologne had a sharp clean smell. It was diluted with distilled water, hence the name toilet water, which Beth used only in the mornings.

At last, the maid was finished. The door closed quietly behind her.

'Good,' Florrie said, joining Beth and Justin at the main window. The view, even in the fading light, had the grandeur of formal well-manicured grass and edges. It stretched as far as the eye could see.

'Wait till you see it in the morning, Justin. It's just spectacular,' Beth said.

'Can't wait,' Justin said.

At this, both Beth and Florrie laughed.

'Men! No sense of the more delicate things in life,' Beth said, throwing up her arms in despair. She was happy at this moment.

'Now freshen up and come down for dinner; you'll hear the gong quite clearly. We have much to discuss regarding the Feltsham family, do we not?'

'So you've heard then?' Beth said.

'I have, Beth. James will be joining us and he wants to apologise and explain how Algernon Feltsham and his sister came to be on the invitation list.'

'Oh no, Florrie!'

'I'm afraid so, my dear.'

'Now try to rest and I'll see you both later.'

When she had gone, Beth turned to Justin. 'So it all follows us, my dear. I'm so sorry.'

Justin smiled. 'We'll see it through together, my love. Don't upset yourself.'

Beth sighed; it was going to be a difficult weekend, if Feltsham raised the matter.

# CHAPTER 6

Lord James Albert Augustus Hastings stood six foot two with the presence and bearing only centuries of power and privilege can produce. He rose from the table to greet them.

'So glad you could come. It's so very good of you, given the circumstances, which I regret I have added too,' he said, kissing Beth lightly on the cheek and shaking Justin's hand.

They both liked James, for they had spent many happy times together over the years. James was godfather to their son Edward and a steadfast friend.

'I am sure there is a good explanation, James, for we know you so well. What brought it about?'

'As you know, Florrie normally handles all the invitations. This time, because the baby is soon due, I asked my office clerk to let the staff deal with it. I added to the list by inviting my board of directors from a number of companies I own. The list stands at one hundred and forty guests altogether,' Lord James said, taking a short breath before continuing. 'Among them is a well-known finance house that I have controlling shares in. Running my eyes down the invitation list, which I should have done sooner, there was his name and that of his sister. To withdraw the invitation was far too late, and really very difficult.'

There was a long pause. 'Can you forgive me?' Then he added, 'Florrie can't, of course,' he said in a solemn voice.

Justin spoke first. 'James, after all these years, of course we forgive you. Is that not so, Beth?'

Beth leaned across the table and held James's hand. 'Of course we do.'

Lord James looked grateful. 'Again, I'm so very sorry. But let us be positive in this matter, he may not bring it up at such a social gathering.'

Justin nodded, but not convincingly. 'Indeed, let us hope that is the case.'

'Now let us enjoy our dinner and this time we have together,' Florence said.

So the evening passed.

The morning brought a clear bright beginning-of-June sky, if a little chilly. After breakfast, Beth and Justin strolled in the garden and inspected the stables until a light lunch was served. At four o'clock, tea with cucumber sandwiches and cakes were placed on a table on the front lawn.

Lord James joined them. 'Sorry I missed you both at breakfast but, an estate to run, cottage rents and fences to be repaired. Some extra help for tonight in the kitchens is needed as well. My estate manager Williams, is a very good man, but he can't make all the necessary decisions. I'm not here often these days, what with business commitments in London when I stay at my club in St James's. It's where I first heard Lord Feltsham talk in a loud voice about his uncle and how he had been deceived by a scoundrel and an impostor out of all of his wealth in Sydney. Then he escaped to New Zealand where he tried to rebuild his life while helping the Maori to find homesteads.'

Beth jumped to her feet. 'The bloody man sold them plots of land that never existed. When the Maori chiefs found out, they buried him face down in a grave in Dunedin.'

Florence placed a gentle hand on Beth's shoulder. 'There, there, my dear don't upset yourself so. We'll speak no more about the bloody man.'

Lady Florence said, before blushing a deep red, 'See what comes of one when one befriends an Australian.'

The laughter that broke out eased the tension. Sandwiches were eaten and tea drunk. 'Johnson,' called Lord James.

'Sir?'

'Go to the cellar and open a bottle of that dessert wine we like. The what's it called…?'

'The Commandaria, but I regret there are only a few bottles remaining, sir!'

'Then hurry to serve it, Johnson, for we need to take the taste of the bloody man off of our tongues. And then apologise to the maid for our bad language.'

Another burst of laughter came from them all

'Of course, sir,' Johnson said, a slight smile around his lips.

When the wine was served with great ceremony by Johnson, Lord James raised his glass. 'To a successful evening with no accusations from that bl…y man.'

Glasses clinked to a chorus of, 'To a successful evening.'

To say the Grand Ballroom was vast was an understatement in the extreme. The marble floor gleamed bright and smooth; it reflected the lights from the overhead chandeliers, of which there were three lines running the length of the room. The walls hung with silk and decorated flowers, the whole scene was alight with joyful expectation of the coming evening.

Lady Florence was in deep conversation with the planning committee who had been charged with all the arrangement of seating charts, foods to be served and the all-important music programme, which was composed of dances where the young people could meet hopefully their prospective husbands and wives.

'Well done, gentlemen, you have excelled yourselves.'

A collective bow came from the committee. 'Thank you, Lady Florence,' said a distinguished older man who had served the house of Hastings for many years.

Lord and Lady Hastings stood at the main doors to the ballroom as the master of ceremonies announced the guests by name, social standing and rank, while their hosts greeted each one in turn, a tiresome part of the evening but an essential one.

The MC, a former guardsman, straightened his back.

'General Sir Markus Winterstone.'

'General, what a pleasure to see you again,' Lady Florence said.

'Good of you to invite me, Lady Hastings.'

So it continued for another forty minutes. Some guests later, the MC announced, 'Lord Feltsham and Lady Cordelia Feltsham.'

Florence held out her hand. Lord Feltsham took it in his ungloved one. The MC stepped forward but Lord Hastings was already in front of Feltsham.

'My lord, I see you have forgotten your gloves. Let me arrange for a pair to be found for you.'

'Never wear them, sir,' he said in a slightly slurred voice. 'Like to feel the soft touch of the female guests.'

'Not in this house, sir.' Adding, 'Johnson.'

'Sir.'

'A pair of gloves for Lord Feltsham please.'

'Very good, sir.'

'Indulge me, Lord Algernon, I beg you.'

With a line of guests behind him he said, 'If you insist.'

'I do, my dear chap, I do.'

Unsteadily, and resting on Cordelia's arm, Feltsham made his way into the ballroom.

'Not a good start, my dear. I'll have Johnson watch him.'

Florence sighed then turned to the next guest. 'How nice to see you both again.'

Finally, all the guests were assembled.

The orchestra began to tune up their respective instruments in preparation of the march down the centre of the floor allowing everyone to see who was present. It was led by Lord and Lady Hastings with great fanfare and pomp.

Florence looked regal in a loose-fitting black gown, while Beth stood tall and imperious in her Rococo gown. The men, all in black, were wearing fitted dress coats with matching trousers. The outfit was made complete with black or coloured waistcoats decorated with gold buttons over white dress shirts with neckties although, some of the younger men were wearing the new fashionable cravats. Their soft leather boots shone black in sharp contrast to their white gloves.

So the scene was set, a Viennese Waltz began the evening's music. The straight backs of the men and the swish of the brightly coloured gowns had the dowagers chattering in their seats around the dance floor.

Anterooms to the left of the ballroom were being used by the ladies, assisted by two maids in each room, to adjust the gowns after their travel and any necessary hair styles that needed some slight adjustments.

On the other side stood footmen at tables of food and punch bowls, a glass of which was already firmly in Lord Algernon's now white-gloved hand.

It was ten o'clock when the orchestra began a lively polka.

Feltsham staggered out of the side room onto the edge of the dance floor bumping into a young man. As he did, both the glass and its contents found their way to the marble floor.

'You imbecile, look what you've done.'

'I was just standing here, sir.'

Beth, who was standing near the young man, looked at Lord Feltsham in disgust.

'This is what happens when you attend a ball filled with unsuitable guests. The daughters of convicts and impostors,' Feltsham said, in a loud voice, to a man at his side.

The man looked at him and walked away. 'Unsuitable indeed, sir, and drunk, sir.'

Seeing Beth close by, Feltsham grabbed her arm and began to dance. 'I'm sure you're familiar to dancing with many men,' Feltsham said, in a slurred voice.

'Take your hands off of me, you stupid drunken slob.' The powerful slap to his face sent Feltsham reeling across the dance floor into a set of tables and chairs. Beth stood over him, clenched fists at her side, daring him to get up. Feltsham didn't move.

Johnson hurried into a side room and spoke into Lord Hastings ear, 'It's Lord Feltsham, sir.'

# CHAPTER 7

'What seems to be the difficulty, Lord Feltsham?'

'This ill-mannered, inbred lout pushed me, and your undesirable guest slapped me, sir.'

'Sir, I was just st...'

'Robert, I'll see to this please go to the orchestra end of the ballroom and stay there. I'll speak to you later. Beth are you alright?'

Beth nodded. Florrie was at her side shaking her head.

'Johnson, bring Edwards and escort his lordship to my study where we can speak in private.'

'Sir.'

'Ladies and gentlemen, apologies for the slight interruption. Conductor, a lively gallop, if you would please?'

Beckoning Sir Justin to follow him, he walked purposefully but slowly towards his study.

Inside, Edwards was holding Feltsham in a vice-like grip.

'Unhand me at once. Unless you want a whip taken to you.'

Edwards smiled a slow, meaningful smile. 'Now, now, sir, there's a good gentleman. We'll soon have you comfortable.'

The door closed silently behind them, leaving Edwards outside to ensure no one else went into the study.

Carefully lighting a cigar, Lord Hastings turned to Feltsham in a cloud of smoke.

'Now, sir what is on your troubled mind that justifies upsetting my guests?'

'You invite it sir, by your invitation to unsuitable guests.'

'I am aware sir, of the rumours you are spreading. A so-called impostor that allegedly defrauded your uncle out of his money in Sydney. So, let us get to the point: you do not bring these accusations to my home. Do I make myself clear? If not then my man Edwards will call for your carriage.'

'You defend this man against one of your own class?'

'I know the full story, sir, and this man you speak of was given a royal pardon by Her Majesty for his good service to the people and the economy of Australia.'

'Her Majesty was misinformed by her advisers, something I intend to put right both here and in Sydney.'

'Not from my ballroom, in my house, while availing yourself of my hospitality.'

'You would rather extend that hospitality to the daughter of a convict and scoundrel who sets herself up as one of us rather than the trollop she is?' Feltsham said, red in the face with temper and drink.

At this, Sir Justin stepped forward. He grabbed Feltsham by the lapels of his coat. 'How dare you speak of my wife in such terms, or lay your hands upon her.' Then, removing his left glove, he struck Feltsham across the face.

'My seconds will call on you in the morning to set a time and place. I'll see you face down in the mud of Hampstead Heath.'

'Justin wait, please. Lord Feltsham will apologise for his drunken remark, is that not so, sir?'

'Dammed if I will! If it's a duel you are after, Standish, I'll accommodate you.'

'Call for my carriage. I have no wish to stay longer.'

'That, sir, is certainly something I am most pleased to accommodate,' Lord Hastings said.

'Edwards.'

The door opened in a rush of music and cigar smoke. 'Sir.'

'Lord Feltsham is leaving.'

'Very well, sir. This way my lord. Lady Cordelia is also ready to leave.'

Turning to Sir Justin, Feltsham said, 'Day after tomorrow, will that suit you?'

'Perfectly.'

Stepping out of the study, Lord Hastings called Johnson to him.

'Please ask Lady Hastings and Lady Standish to join us, there's a good chap.'

'Very good, sir,' Johnson said, a grim look on his face.

'No, no I'll not have it, you can't be serious. A duel in this day and age? Why it's 1879,' Beth said, in the cutting edge of a now-strong Australian accent. 'The bloody man's not worth it.'

'But your good name is, my dear, and I'll not have such a remark made about you, and that's final.'

Beth threw her arms around him. 'You romantic old bonzer.'

Florence burst into tears. 'I don't know what that means, but it sounds absolutely right.'

Lord Hastings took Justin by the hand. 'Your second, at your service.'

'Thank you, James.'

It was four o'clock in the morning before the ball finished. An army of servants swept into the ballroom to clear up, while the guests departed and Florrie, James, Justin and Beth prepared to retire to bed.

Firstly, James gathered them at the foot of the stairs. 'A late breakfast, then we make plans to return to London where we begin the duelling arrangements for the next day.'

'Yes, and we'll all stay at our Portman Square house of course,' Justin said.

'Excellent, and for the evening we can book rooms at the Spaniards Inn on the Heath. The ladies will remain at Portman Square.'

At this, Beth bridled. 'I intend to be there James,' she said, in a flat tone.

'Not possible my dear,' Justin said, adding, 'This is a men-only affair.'

Beth bristled with indignation. 'In Sydney I would have attended, as I did, bare-knuckle fights and any other sporting event.'

'We're not in Australia, my dear; we are in London and this is not a sporting event. It's just not done here, or anywhere else in Europe for that matter. Please leave this to me,' Justin said, in a firm voice.

Lord Hastings motioned to Johnson.

'Sir.'

'Have Lady Hastings' maid pack clothes for a few days, three at most, and she will attend her ladyship in London. Then go to the armoury and have my grandfather's duelling pistols ready for the morning.'

'Very well, sir.'

'That's most decent of you, James. Are you sure? For I have pistols in London, not the finest but very good.'

'Nonsense these are a matched set with excellent balance and weight, which you can judge for yourself at breakfast. Now let's try to get some sleep.'

Come morning in the breakfast room, after what all agreed was a restless night, they served themselves from the silver tureens of porridge, scrambled eggs, kedgeree, toast with jam, and hot tea.

When finished, Lord Hastings turned to Johnson. 'Thank you, Johnson. Give our apologies to Cook for our lateness and lack of doing justice to her cooking this morning. Also, would you bring the pistols to the table for Sir Justin to examine?'

'Very well, my lord.'

'Oh! And have the carriages ready for our departure in about two hours.'

'Already in hand sir.'

'Good man.'

Johnson placed the pistol case in front of Justin.

Beth visibly shuddered. 'Florrie, what are we doing?'

'Entertaining the field of honour, my dear. The portrait at the top of the main stairs is, as you know, that of James's father. The one leading to the west wing is James's grandfather; you'll see he only has one arm. James, will you tell the story?'

James, a cup of tea in hand, began to relate the story. 'In 1795 my grandfather, while in Paris, had a falling out with a French nobleman over the battle of Agincourt. He was challenged to a duel. Through a friend he bought these Nicolas Noel Boutet, single-shot, flintlock, rifled .58 calibre pistols.'

Beth leaned forward. 'Why are the barrels blue?'

'To prevent glare, when sighting,' Justin said.

'Indeed, and they are among the very best ever made,' said James.

Beth looked at the present Lord Hastings. 'What was the outcome of the duel, James?'

'Before my grandfather left Paris, he placed flowers on the nobleman's grave.'

'Is this what we intend to do? And you think Australians are barbaric.'

'A question of honour, my dear, among gentlemen.'

For heartbeats no one spoke. Breaking the silence, Beth said, 'Don't misunderstand me, shoot the bloody man by all means, but don't put fancy words to it. In Sydney an out-and-out bastard is just that; we don't dress it up with words of honour. We put a scratch mark on the ground and get on with it.'

James smiled. 'I understand, my dear, for he has already caused you much heartache and upset, but different cultures, different mores. However, the result will be the same and he may well desist from going further.'

'Do you believe that, Justin?' Beth said.

'Let us hope so.'

Beth stood up. 'If I were a man, I'd beat the hell out of him and bugger the field of honour.'

They all laughed, even Johnson.

'We are becoming Australianised, Johnson.'

'Indeed, sir.' Then he added, 'If you'd allow me to say, sir, I hope all goes well, Sir Standish.'

'Thank you Johnson.'

# CHAPTER 8

The journey to London was one of subdued silence in both carriages. The duelling case of pistols lay on Justin's lap, a constant reminder of what lay ahead.

Beth placed her hand upon his. 'I'm sorry to have brought this about, Justin.'

'This is not of your making my dear, but that of Algernon Feltsham.'

'How do you proceed?'

'I will send a written challenge to Feltsham today to be delivered by James as my second. He will demand an apology. If not given, then the duel goes ahead. A time and place will be agreed, a judge appointed to rule and ensure the duel is conducted in keeping with the strict regulations of a duel.'

Beth gave a long sigh of resignation. 'Where and when will it take place?'

'Tomorrow morning at 5am on Hampstead Heath, if Feltsham is agreeable. No reason why not, for it's close at hand for us both. I'll stay at the Spaniards Inn tonight. A flat piece of ground will be found by the seconds with no irregular ground around it and reasonably close to a house or inn if required by either principals in the event of serious wounds. However, a doctor will be in attendance at the duel. So there's no need to worry,' Justin said, resting his hand upon Beth's.

'Not worry, not worry? Dear God this is madness, Justin.'

'It is set in motion, Beth, and unless he retracts what he's said then it will go ahead. He cannot make these remarks about you.'

'But at what cost?'

'That will be decided on the field of honour,' Justin said, in a flat tone.

By late afternoon they were at Portman Square. Maids and footmen were putting the guest room ready for Florrie and James while a light meal was being prepared in the kitchens. Thomas the head butler laid out Sir Justin's clothes for the morning with a grim look upon his face and much shaking of his head. Molly saw to the children by taking them to bed early, but not before Justin gave them both a tight squeeze for what seemed a rather long time; they all understood.

'See you in the morning, Father,' called Edward over his shoulder.

At this, Beth placed her head in her hands.

After the meal, which was hardly eaten, Lord Hastings left for Feltsham's club with the letter from Sir Justin Standish, all formal, enveloped and complete with a wax seal. Rooms were booked at the Spaniards Inn. By evening all was in place. Feltsham had refused to apologise. The duel was arranged.

Beth wanted to at least come with them to the Spaniards Inn.

'Please, Beth, I must keep my mind on the morning.'

'I understand, Beth, how you feel, but Justin is right,' Florrie said.

'I know, I know, but nevertheless.'

'They also serve who sit and wait, Beth, and we will do that with fortitude and strength, will we not?'

'If I could just get my hands around that bloody man's neck,' Beth said, holding her hands out in front of her.

The time came for Justin and James to leave. The difficult farewells were made harder by the night air and the closing of the big doors, then the carriage rattled off into the chilly night towards the Heath.

Beth and Florrie settled down to a long nerve-shredding night.

The Spaniards Inn was alight with the evening's bawdy entrainment and drinking. At the furthest end of the long bar, Feltsham stood glaring at Justin while his second negotiated his way through the crowd with drinks in his hand. Jostled by a man coming the other way, he was about to remonstrate with him, then thought better of it given the man's size and demeanour.

'Who you fucking pushing?'

'Sorry, my fault I'm sure.'

'Do you see them?' Feltsham said. 'Standish and his second, Lord Hastings? They'll be reprimanded over this both in the Palace of Westminster and the House of Lords; duelling has been illegal for some time, so that's something.'

'So will you be, Algernon. Is that not so?'

'I don't care, to smear them is worth it.'

The landlord stepped from behind the bar. 'Your rooms are ready, sirs, top of the stairs first on the right.'

'We're not near, Sir Standish are we?'

'No, my lord, they're on the top floor. Please don't tell what this is about, sirs, for I have no wish to know. The times of Dick Turpin and his father, who was the landlord here at the time, are long over, my lord, and I'm not a curious man.' So saying, he returned to his other customers.

Justin nodded over to them. 'Yes, I see them we'll have a whisky each and then an early night given that we need to be up by four o'clock.'

'Indeed. Landlord, two glasses of your best whisky if you would.'

'I have some Dewar's, sir, if that's to your liking?'

'It is indeed,' Justin said.

The morning came soon enough, misty and chilly. The Heath was still, the day struggling to begin, but losing.

Sir Fredrick Plummer came forward. 'Good morning, gentlemen. The other principal is already here. I trust you are satisfied that your seconds have chosen me to be the judge in this duel?'

'Your reputation goes ahead of you, Sir Fredrick,' Justin said.

'Appreciated, Sir Standish. Gentlemen, please join me if you will.' The men complied with his request. 'Thank you. Firstly the choice of pistols need to be agreed.'

The respective seconds opened the cases.

'I'll take my own,' Feltsham said.

The judge examined it. 'Very well, Sir Standish?'

'I'll also take my own.'

'Gentlemen, we are agreed, the seconds can now charge the pistols.'

While this was being done, Sir Fredrick turned to the principals. 'Now to the rules, gentlemen.

'You will stand back to back, pistols held high above you.

'I will count ten paces. When complete, you will stand still.

'I will call out: turn, aim, fire.

'Is that understood?'

Both nodded.

'Finally, can I persuade either of you to withdraw the remarks made or injuries inflicted and thereby call the duel off?'

'No.'

'No.'

'So be it. Gentlemen, your places.'

When they were back to back, Feltsham whispered over his shoulder, 'I'm going to kill you, Standish.'

Justin said nothing.

'Eyes to the front,' called Sir Fredrick.

For heartbeats all was silent.

'One, two, three, four, five, six, seven, eight, nine.'

A shot rang out. Birds flew from their nestlings. The gunshot echoed into the dawn-shadowed light.

Justin, his back still turned, fell to the ground. A streak of blood ran down his left sleeve.

The doctor ran forward. Lord Hastings shouted foul.

Sir Fredrick walked over to Feltsham. 'You are a cheat, sir. Stand where you are.'

'I thought I heard you say ten.'

'A flesh wound only, thank goodness,' said the doctor.

The judge walked slowly over to Sir Justin, as he did, he said very clearly and loudly, 'Ten.'

With great dignity Sir Justin Standish turned.

Again in a loud voice the judge said, 'Your shot, sir.'

Feltsham dropped to his knees, throwing his pistol down. 'Wait, wait this is murder I am unarmed and defenceless. My second will vouch for it and bear witness. Is that not so?' Feltsham said, turning to his second.

He was one of Feltsham's gambling cronies but he was not about to commit social suicide.

'Vouch for what, my lord?'

'That this is cold-blooded murder, man.'

'I am here to second you in a duel, sir, which I am ready to continue with.'

Sir Justin, standing sideways, his pistol in his outstretched hand, slowly took aim.

Feltsham, his hands out in front of him, cowered away.

'Stand still, Lord Feltsham. Sir Standish, aim and fire.'

A shot again broke the silence of the morning. The ball spun its way skywards as Sir Standish shot into the air.

'You are not worth the powder, sir.' Holding the pistol barrel first, he passed it to James. 'Your pistol, Lord Hastings, and thank you.

'Gentlemen, my appreciation for your understanding and honourable service during this duel. Lord Hastings, could you please assist me to our carriage for I feel slightly faint?' By now his left arm was covered in blood.

The doctor made a sling to support the weight of the arm, then they slowly made their way to the waiting carriage.

Behind them, Feltsham called out, 'It's not the end of this matter. I now have humiliation to add to your debt to me.' He stood there alone, while the mist lifted into the dawn sky. Everyone had left him, including his second.

# CHAPTER 9

'Dear God! Justin!'

'I'm alright. Thomas, get me a clean white shirt before the children are down.'

'Sir.'

Beth called out for Molly.

'Yes, Beth,' Molly said, looking in alarm at Justin.

'Keep the children upstairs until I call them.'

'Right.' Shirt in hand, Thomas began to cut the old shirt away.

'Leave it,' said Beth 'I'll do that. Glad at last to be doing something after the long nights wait. Please send a runner around to our doctor immediately. Telling him the urgency of the matter.'

Florrie wanted to know all that had happened as she brought Justin a glass of brandy.

Clean shirt on, Justin sat back on the settee that a maid had covered with a dark sheet while James related the whole episode of the morning's duel.

'The bloody, bloody man. Sorry, Mary,' said Beth to the parlour maid.

'I agree, my lady. Oh sorry!'

The remark broke the tension. The front doorbell rang out, and Thomas hurried to open it.

Doctor Benton said nothing but moved quickly to Justin's side.

'Ladies, would you please be good enough to leave us for a moment,' he said, beginning to remove the shirt.

The flesh wound was deep and long but had not damaged the bone. Looking up, the doctor said, 'The "round" has torn some muscle and it will be some weeks in the healing. Do not tell me how this came about; I do not wish to know, but it is, of course, a bullet wound and I should make a report. I do not have my report sheets with me and probably can't find them at my surgery.'

'Thank you Oliver,' said Justin, as the doctor began to clean the wound then placed a sling around Justin's neck.

'I'll see you again in the morning. These tablets will help to ease the pain, together with a small brandy.'

'Can I offer you a drink, Doctor?'

'I trust you're not trying to bribe me, Sir Standish.'

'You know me better than that, Oliver.'

'In that case, a small whisky to keep out the cold,' he said in his warm Irish brogue.

The ladies returned. Beth's anguished voice addressed the doctor.

'Will he be alright, Doctor Benton?'

'Well now haven't I been treating him since he was born? In fact it was my very self who brought him into this troubled world and that's a fact. Why he's had worse injuries than this on the playing fields of Eton. And they certainly cost more than my fee will be. Now don't go telling me how it happened for we have been over that, so we have,' he said downing his drink in one experienced satisfying gulp.

The door closed after the doctor while a small amount of London fog crept into the hall. It was late morning. For heartbeats no one spoke. Then the children burst in and all was laughter and shouting.

'What has happened to your arm, Father? You look like one of my tin soldiers after Waterloo.'

'Can I be nurse, Father?' said Effie.

'Of course you can and how fortunate I am to have such a pretty nurse, but I am not as brave as your Waterloo infantryman, Edward. It's just a small accident, my nurse and Doctor Benton will soon make it better.'

A game of cards and the children's chatter brought them to seven o'clock. Molly came sweeping into the drawing room. 'Time for bed so it is, say goodnight to everyone.'

Kisses all round and, finally, peace reigned again in the room.

Beth turned to Florrie. 'See what you have let yourself in for having all these children?'

'If they are like Effie and Edward, we will be well pleased.'

'Thank you but you need to rest now, we all do. How is the arm, my dear?'

'As if I'd been at Waterloo.'

The day ended in laughter, all were aware it could have been so much worse. However, the following morning brought a letter addressed to Sir Justin Standish. It was wax sealed and delivered by hand.

Justin read it out loud:

*Jessup, Jessup and Montague (Solicitors)*
*June the Sixth, 1879*

*Chambers Address*
*122B Marylebone Road,*
*London NW1*

*Dear Sir,*

*I have the task of advising you of Lord Algernon Hugo Feltsham's
intention to take you to court for slander and holding his name
in contempt.*

*We would be obliged if you would advise our chambers of your legal
representative to enable us to proceed.*

*Yours sincerely,*
*Signed*

*Joshua Templeman Jessup LLB*

'Damn the man,' Beth said, when Justin had finished.

# CHAPTER 10

'Enough is enough.'

'Meaning?' said Justin.

'We've done it your way, the man's way; now I'll do it a woman's way,' Beth said.

'Wait, Beth, it is your husband's place in London's society to deal with these things.'

Beth placed her hands on the table and drummed her fingers. 'Then, my dear, it's time things changed. All of this is about me and my family. I regret that your family have been so ill treated by this man. The House of Feltsham have caused us great harm. The death of my mother, my father's incarceration in Port Arthur Penal Colony, the attempts on his life and that of his close friend Regan O'Hara who died in their escape from the penal colony: all a direct result of the House of Feltsham, and now the duel and this legal action. No, Justin, I must take the fight to Lord Algernon Hugo Bloody Feltsham. I'm so sorry if this causes further upset to your family, but there it is. That's what comes of marrying a convict's daughter.'

For heartbeats it was silent.

Then Justin smiled. 'The marrying of you was the only thing I've ever got completely right, my darling, and I carry a bullet scar to prove it.'

They fell into each other's arms.

'So what do you intend to do?'

'When I married you, my dear, dear Justin, I was a most fortunate woman, but I became invisible. I was, indeed I am by law, tied hand and foot to you in the eyes of society. No rights, no vote, no say in my or my children's future. But it was I who brought our children into this socially restricted world. And I believe that the hand that rocks the cradle, rocks the world. For our son Edward all is well, but for our daughter, she is committed to the role of a husband's chattel and expected to fit into a social mould of men's making. I know you've heard me speak about this many times, my dear, but now, and in the face of Feltsham's actions, and that of many other men like him to so many other women, the time has come that it must stop. In very many ways, this too is Shenkin's legacy. A right to self-determination, whatever your gender. He believed that and practised it, and since I am determined to fulfil his legacy, I will pursue it to my dying breath.'

'A long speech, my dear, but a steep hill to climb. I will of course support you with everything in my power. So, I repeat again, what do you intend to do?' Justin said, then added, 'By that remark you can see I've already begun.'

'Then I start well, thank you. Firstly, we are agreed that in Victorian England, even in 1879, women are still less than equal. We are regarded by men as emotional and incapable of making rational decisions. Indeed under the law on our wedding day we become subject to the will of our husband; everything we do is under his direction. He has control of our possessions and even our bodies. He is allowed to beat his wife and even rape her if she refuses to have sex. And he can do this without fear of prosecution. If she still refuses sex, then he can have the marriage annulled and the woman becomes homeless, no rights to her own possessions, no access to her children and shunned by society. He can expect to have custody of the children and will always be their legal guardian. In the eyes of society the woman after marriage is the homemaker, the caregiver and is put on a pedestal, a small circle of space in which she can exercise no self-will of her own.'

Beth paused. 'As you know, Justin, this is why I joined the women's feminist movement, to fight for equality in education, work and the electoral rights to a vote. Most of us in high society are still regrettably class conscious, but theoretically we believe all women make up a single force and object most strongly to being oppressed purely on the basis of our sex. For the poor it is much worse; I see it daily in the East End, Justin. Reform on child labour is needed, safety in the mines and factories, something that Shenkin felt so strongly about, public health and a final end to slavery in the British Empire.'

'A tall order, my dear, one that I would be hesitant to put forward to the front benches of the House of Commons. But I can make a start, I'll ask for a petition from my constituency to sound out the general feeling.'

Beth smiled. 'A steep uphill climb indeed, my dear, but it must start somewhere. It will put me in the glare of social attention and from that platform I will confront the House of Feltsham too.'

# CHAPTER 11

The Women's Movement hall was full of women and children. Beth stood at the front reading from her notes.

'If we are to bring about change, then we must act as one voice against the injustices to women and to that of our children. Today we have with us Mary Walters, a young woman married to an abusive husband. She talks here today at great risk to herself, her marriage and to her future.'

'Mary please,' Beth said, ushering Mary forward.

'I'm not a speaker like Lady Standish, I'm afraid, so I hope you can all hear me clearly at the back,' she said, then, taking a deep breath, she began.

It came out in a rush of words. 'I was married five years ago. At the beginning my husband was attentive, but this soon changed once I had born a child in the second year. Alfred would stay out late, refuse to help in the care of our young daughter. If the child cried at night, he would blame me and hit me, until in the end I slept downstairs with our daughter Violet. I never know what he earns. I am given just enough to scrape by on. In that second year, he began to drink heavily. He comes home in a rage ready to hit me for not having his dinner ready or refusing to have sex with him, at which time he always threatens me with divorce and that he'd throw me out onto the streets.'

At this a woman stood up. 'That sounds like my old man that does. I've gone through that many times.'

Then another voice from the floor shouted out, 'Me too.'

'And me,' said a woman at the very back of the hall. 'Locked in a bleeding room I was for three days with split lips and a black eye. Go to the police and what do they say? "He's your husband he is, so put up with it." Bastards all of them and we have no say at all.'

In the front row, a well-dressed woman stood up. Dressed in the latest fashion of an expensive well-cut, decorated bustle skirt that draped full at the back and was embellished with ribbons and lace, she held her head high, her hair piled up on top of her head. On top of which sat a broad-brimmed hat attached to which was a most beautiful peacock feather that bobbed up and down to every movement she made. In a clear firm voice, that had a very slight accent, she said, 'Me too and I wish to make an announcement.'

The woman to the left of Beth whispered into her ear.

Beth stood up. 'It's Lady Trellis I understand; is that not right?'

'As was, yes, but a title I no longer use since my divorce from Sir Charles Trellis some years ago. Following the divorce I have been out of the country for some while. I return from time to time to visit my sister.' Without hesitation she continued, 'Now as to my statement.'

'Please, Lady Trellis, you have the floor.'

'Abusive husbands are not restricted to the poorer classes, far from it, indeed they are at all levels of society. My younger sister and I were in finishing school here in London when we met out husbands. Naïve head strong and far from home, we went ahead with the weddings, much to our parents' later dismay. Our husbands demanded dowries from us and confiscated all that we had in the way of possessions and assets here in London. They had been in public school together: gamblers, drunkards, womanisers and cheats the pair of them. I found this out on the very day and night of my marriage, bringing me to my senses, if too late, in the most abrupt way. On that day, at that time on that night, I stood in the bedroom and refused to consummate the marriage with a drunken sot.

'To say he struck me was to put too fine a word on it; he beat me until I was nothing more than a broken and bloody rag doll. It brought servants to the room who were both shocked and dismayed at the sight. They were at a loss as to what to do. Sir Charles screamed at them to get out. A week later, with me still recovering from the beating, he had the marriage annulled and threw me out, keeping everything I had brought to the marriage. A good friend from our finishing school took me in and nursed me until I was well, for which I will forever be grateful.

My sister experienced a great deal worse, I regret to say. She was only seventeen at the time. Her husband returned home one evening drunk and wanted sex. When my sister refused, he beat her violently, resulting in a fractured skull and broken jaw. It sent her into a coma, which she is still in. He arranged for her to go into a private sanatorium, to hush things up. She does not know me, or where she is. She just sits on her bed and rocks to and fro. He will not divorce her in case the truth comes out. As a family we have no legal redress; she was his wife, his chattel.'

Lady Trellis paused for a moment. For heartbeats all was still. Then she turned to the body of people in the hall. 'I commit myself to the service of this women's movement. To that end, I wish to make a donation of £250 pounds sterling on this and every quarter from this day forward.'

A gasp went up from the assembled crowd. Lady Trellis continued, 'Is it not time to change this society, this barbaric law, and place women on an equal standing with men? A strong wave of feminism will do it. Withdraw our supportive roles in life: caring, nurturing, running their homes, bearing their children, until we are heard.'

By now the whole room was in an uproar.

Beth raised her hands in the air. 'Quiet, quiet, please.'

When it became quieter, Beth turned to Lady Trellis. 'That is a great deal of money, Lady Trellis, and a strong speech to match it, one that I am in much agreement with. However, the law is on the side of the men in this man's world. Withdraw our supportive roles, that could be effective, but it would also publicly polarise the genders and we are looking for equality not isolation, are we not?'

'We are, I agree. But I feel you are in favour of a more direct approach, are you not?'

A few hands went up in the audience from a number of women; two of whom were trying to hold their children still but losing the fight.

'Yes! One on one, in fact a very personal and private approach, Lady Trellis,' Beth said.

'I'm all ears, Lady Standish, as I am sure the gathering is.'

'We are! let's hear it!' came a chorus of voices.

Beth raised her arms for quiet. 'Well, ladies how far are we prepared to go?'

'Whatever it takes or why are we here?' called a woman from the back.

Beth nodded, as did Lady Trellis.

'To begin with,' said Beth, 'the fight against a male-dominated society is not new. In the fifth century, some four hundred years before the birth of Christ, the Peloponnesian war between Athens and Sparta had been raging for twenty years. The women were bearing sons who were dying on the battlefields between the two cities. A mother called Lysistrata brought the women of Athens together; they took control of the Acropolis where there was a chest of money held. They refused to budge unless their men sued for peace. The men refused, so Lysistrata sent women to Sparta and joined forces with its women who were of a like mind'.

A more direct approach was suggested, a very personal one. No sex with their husbands or lovers on both sides until the men sued for peace.

The very thought jolted the male population into a reconsideration of the war. Publicly the men decided the war was not benefiting either side, that grounds needed to be found to reconcile their differences; they did, but there was no mention of sex. Beth gave a soft smile. 'I am not suggesting we go that far, but a jolt is needed. A whisper in the ear at the appropriate moment, so to speak. About how strongly we feel in this unequal society.'

Lady Trellis began the applause and stood up.

'Lady Trellis.'

'Firstly, I no longer use that title; my name is Maria Romero Alvarez. My sister is Paloma Romero Alvarez. We are Argentinean, my family home is in Buenos Aires where my people are cattle-ranchers with a number of ranches in the Pampas area. They are committed to righting the wrong done to their daughters here in London, hence the money.'

'Miss Alvarez…'

'Maria please.'

Beth smiled. It is what she would have said. 'As you are now our main patron would you please join us here on stage, where all can see you.'

Maria Romero Alvarez stood up and mounted the six short steps to the stage. A roar of approval and clapping greeted her.

'Thank you, Maria. Please be seated. I'll make the introductions to your fellow committee members later.'

'Good of you, Lady Standish.'

'Beth please.' They both laughed.

'Beth of course.'

'I also wish to speak to you privately after the meeting, if that's possible, Beth?'

'My pleasure, my dear, my pleasure.'

After statements were taken from the more graphic experiences of some of the women present, the meeting was finally closed. Chairs stacked; cups, saucers and plates washed then put into the kitchen ready for the next meeting.

At last Beth introduced Maria to her fellow committee members, all profusely thanked her for her generous donation.

When only Beth and Maria stood facing one another Beth let out a sigh.

The dark flashing eyes of Maria Romero Alvarez held her stare. 'You have my full support, not only financially but in the running and organising of the Women's Movement while you are away in Sydney.'

'I'm going to Sydney?'

'Of course you are, to stop Lord Feltsham spreading further slanderous lies about your father.'

'I can't believe the rumours have reached Buenos Aires,' Beth said, with an incredulous look upon her face.

'I follow everything the man does for I have serious reason to. Both him and his wife.'

'You are mistaken, Maria, Lord Feltsham is not married.'

'Oh but he is.'

'You are misinformed, my dear, and why would it be of any interest to you anyway?'

'Because his wife is my sister Paloma, who he put into an asylum. Regrettably, as I said, he refuses to divorce her for fear of the truth coming out. I offer this information to you that the time may come that you can use it against him, I have all the necessary paperwork to prove it.'

# CHAPTER 12

'But that's incredible, Beth. Do you know which institution she is in? It needs to be verified,' Justin said.

'No she wants to, with my help, discredit Feltsham and get the marriage annulled without further upset to her sister. Paloma which means "dove" is a sensitive, nervous and highly strung woman. This, together with the physical abuse she received at the hands of Feltsham, renders her a broken woman.'

'I understand, but how does she feel you can assist her?'

'By bringing Feltsham into the glare of public opinion via his scandalous lies about my father both here and in Sydney. Once done, she will confront him with his hushed-up marriage and demand a divorce.'

'A tall order, my dear, as we know,' Justin said.

'Indeed. But first, how did your meeting with the solicitors go?'

'They believe Feltsham has no grounds to bring an action without sworn statements from witnesses, and given the fact that duelling is now illegal, that would be difficult to do, so it would be thrown out of court.'

'So?'

'So they recommend we do nothing. If he takes it further, we could bring a counter-charge against Feltsham.'

'I see. Well, let us hope that is the end of it.'

Justin nodded his head. 'Let's hope so. But to something more important at the moment. I have a very good friend in the House of Lords who tells me his lordship is planning to leave for Sydney, together with his sister Cordelia, in September. He will only wait for the summer recess to begin, then leave.'

'Damn the man.'

'You need to be there, Beth, to counter any smear campaign he starts about Shenkin. My father will assist, of course, but at his age I don't want to bring any stress to him or my mother. They intend to come back to England as soon as their sheep station is sold and their Australian assets liquidated.'

'Yes, of course, and there's your sister to be considered too.'

'Indeed the riding accident has placed an unforeseen burden on them.'

'Yes indeed. However, I do have some good news; Florrie has given birth to a healthy baby boy, seven pounds six ounces, to be called Arthur, and we are invited to the christening in ten days. I must be there of course. But I can begin making arrangements to go to Sydney in the meantime. Can you find out how Feltsham intends to sail to Sydney and exactly when.'

'I'll speak to my friend tomorrow.'

The small parish church was full to the rafters with family, friends and the Hastings' servants who had been given the day off to celebrate the occasion.

Flags and bunting crossed the village streets and a band of the local scouts group played music in the square. Lady Hastings arrived in a pony and trap with little Arthur wrapped in a Union Jack flag. The late June sun shone brightly as Lord James Albert Augustus Hastings stood proudly at the gated archway entrance to the church. A small dog joined in the moment with some excited barking as the vicar, the Reverend Archibald Willis, strode down the church path to the sweeping swish of his black cassock and a broad smile upon his face.

'A suitable morning for the ceremony, milord.'

'Indeed, Vicar, let's hope his life continues in the same vein.'

'Amen to that.'

'The young gentleman has arrived accompanied by Lady Hastings,' the vicar said. A cry came from baby Arthur at his dismay of being disturbed from his sleep by a roar from all the assembled guests, but nothing like the scream he gave when the cold blessed water was splashed over his head.

'A fine pair of lungs, milord, do I hear a charge in it?'

'Let's hope not, Vicar. We have enough portraits of ancestors in uniforms already,' Lady Hastings said.

'Quite so, thoughtless of me, please forgive me,' the vicar said, in a rather ruffled voice.

A short walking distance brought them all back to the big house where tables were laid out on the lawns. Baby Arthur was still crying as he was placed into his nanny's concerned arms.

'There now, have they been pouring cold water over you? I don't hold with it. We would have waited longer in chapel than just two weeks before splashing cold wet water around. But nanny will put it right.'

'Sorry, Lily,' Lady Hastings said.

'I have him, off with you now, to your guests isn't it?' she said in her lyrical Welsh accent.

'Florrie he is beautiful and the children seem very pleased with their new brother,' Beth said.

'Hated my sister; she took all my attention away,' said Lord Hastings, smiling broadly.

'We've all made up for it, spoiled is the word I'd use, milord,' said the vicar, in the joyful general mood that pervaded the guests.

'Hear! Hear!' came up from them all.

After the meal and once everyone had said their goodbyes and congratulations were made again, the four of them gathered in the drawing room, the men with brandies in their hands, the women had sloe gin flavoured with berries.

'So, Beth, tell me all the London news.'

'Well, to begin with, Feltsham is preparing for his departure to Sydney where he intends to set up a business syndicate to open a new bank. He has many contacts there from the days when the House of Feltsham made uniforms for the American Civil War at their wool mills in the North of England. The wool came from Australian sheep stations. Shenkin refused to have any part of it. The Feltshams and their partners supplied both sides with uniforms. They also ran the blockade to deliver guns and canon to the south into Virginia, a prominent part of the Confederacy at the time.'

'I've told her she must go before Feltsham spreads his scandalous lies further,' Justin said.

'Yes, you must, Beth. I can take over the running of the feminist movement, and with the good news you told me earlier, of Maria Alvarez's donation, I'm sure we can both continue to move the feminist wave forward ready for your return.'

'Thank you, Florrie. The word is that Feltsham is sailing on the newly built steam propulsion ship that John Elder has built, the *SS Orient*.'

Justin sighed. 'According to the papers she is reputed to be the largest passenger cargo ship to date, apart from the old Great Eastern, and fast despite being iron built. She's driven by the new steam engines with auxiliary barque rig sails. My contact tells me Feltsham is boasting of sailing on her or the *SS Lusitania*, whichever is the quicker, either in September or November via the Cape to Melbourne where, apparently, he has business with sheep station owners who will form part of his syndicate, then on up to Sydney.'

'One of the BKSS Windjammers is scheduled to be in London Docks with a full cargo, for the first time, of frozen beef and mutton in September. I intend to be on it,' Beth said, flatly.

'Given Feltsham will be on the faster steam-driven ship, he'll be there before you, but I don't think there'll be more than a week or two in it, Beth,' James said, pouring them all a nightcap.

The weekend ended both helpfully and hopefully. Beth discussed the ongoing protests of the feminist movement with Florrie and her intention to introduce her to Maria Alvarez before she left for Sydney.

What with all the necessary arrangements that were needed, the time passed swiftly enough, and it soon found Beth, a little tearfully, saying her farewells to the family.

'We'll keep in touch as best we can, Justin. Take care of yourself and the family, oh dear! I feel as if I'm deserting you all.'

'Nonsense, my dear, this must be done, and quickly. Now be on your way; our love goes with you.'

Beth waved from the hansom cab window. She continued to wave as they turned out of Portman Square and headed for London Royal Docks, past the East and West India Docks and into the Victoria Docks area and the much discussed Albert Dock to be opened soon. All was a bustle of activity, shouting men and the crashing of machinery. Dockside cranes were unloading cargo from all over the world into newly built refrigerated warehouses. One of these ships flew the BKSS flag, her cargo of beef and mutton being lifted off and on to the dock side handling areas. Other large ironclad steam ships dwarfed the *Tarn*, the BKSS's sailing ship. Beth made a mental note to discuss the purchase of steam ships with Sir Edward and John Saxon; BKSS must keep ahead of this fast-developing technology if it was to compete with the rest of the world. She felt certain Feltsham would think of this in his challenge to bring BKSS down.

Stepping down from her cab, Beth heard a strong Australian accent shouting orders to the dockside men.

'Careful of those bloody hooks on the ice boxes they're brand new, damn it.'

A foreman shouted back, 'You need better up-to-date lifting equipment, Captain. This is difficult hard work for my men, but we'll take as much care as we can.'

'Appreciate it, Thomson.' Then, lifting his head, he saw Beth alight from the cab together with an Aboriginal dressed in European clothes.

Holding a speaking trumpet to his mouth he called out, 'Please, Lady Standish, be careful.'

The foreman also saw the cab as it turned around. 'Alright, lads take a ten-minute break.'

'Thank you, mate,' called the captain, moving towards the gangplank, while ordering four men to go down to take care of her ladyship's cabin trunks.

Once aboard, Beth looked up at her captain.

'I knew you were arriving, Captain, but how did you know it was me?'

'We passed one of our ships returning to Sydney two weeks ago, and by signal lamps and Columb's dots and dashes we were so advised.'

'The world is advancing at a fast pace, Captain…?'

'Forgive me, Lady Standish. Captain Samuel Harrison at your service. My cabin has been cleared of my things and made ready for you.'

'Harrison, yes I remember. Captain Saxon advised me of your promotion. He thinks very highly of you, Captain.'

'I'll endeavour to live up to it, Lady Standish.'

'I'm sure "Uncle" John also told you I prefer to be called Beth,' she said, holding out her gloved hand. Then, turning, she said, 'This is Tinker, Captain. He'll need a cabin near to me.'

Tinker's smile gave way to the brightest of white teeth; his mane of cotton white hair nodded up and down. 'Pleased to meet you, Captain Harrison.'

'Tinker will also join us for meals.'

'But…'

'This is not negotiable, Captain. Either Tinker is at the table or you won't be.'

'Put that way, Lady Standish, arrangements will be made to accommodate Tinker in every way possible.'

'Thank you, Captain. I felt sure you would see it my way.'

Harrison straightened up to his full height and gave a short, if tight, bow.

'Welcome aboard again. Perhaps you and Tinker would join me this evening for a meal and to raise a glass to a good voyage home.'

'Delighted, Captain, delighted.'

'If you'll forgive me, I must return to the deck to supervise the rest of the unloading and the preparations for loading our return cargo.'

'Till this evening then,' Beth said, taking her first up-close look at her captain.

The captain walked purposefully to the cabin door. He was a tallish man, his peaked captain's hat still in his hand gave view to dark brown wavy hair. He had a tanned sea-weathered face of strong lines. The face was clean shaven and with a ready smile. Beth knew he was only in his early thirties but she could see why John Saxon picked him, for there was a strength in that young face and he had a natural authority. He wore a dark three-quarter jacket held together with four brass buttons, a whitish shirt closed with a black cravat, trousers of the same wool and colour as the jacket, ending in heavy short black boots. Beth liked him.

# CHAPTER 13

The dining mess was a clean but sparsely furnished cabin. However, Beth noted the effort the steward had made in placing a well-laid table of reasonable cutlery and plates with white napkins at the side. The aroma from the galley seemed promising; chicken, thought Beth.

'Good evening, Lady Standish.'

'Beth, may I introduce you to our first mate, Mr Richard Billings.'

A small bristly man stood up. 'Lady Standish, it is indeed a pleasure to meet the owner of the BKSS Shipping Line. My apologies that I was not available to greet you and your companion aboard,' he said, bowing his head to Tinker.

'Pleased to meet you, First Mate,' Tinker said, the broad smile never leaving his coal-black face.

Once seated, the captain said, 'I regret to say we have a problem regarding our departure tomorrow. During loading we discovered damage to the starboard-side tiller chain. An iron bar had got jammed into one of the pulleys damaging it, which now requires repair, meaning we will miss our turnaround time,' Harrison said, adding, 'It is most strange, for the chief engineer tells me it looks as if it's been deliberately tampered with. Do you know of anyone who would want to detain us? Lord Feltsham perhaps?'

'So you know why I'm going to Sydney?'

'Captain Saxon was told by Sir Edward Standish the contents of a letter that arrived the day before our departure. He felt I should be advised in case of any problems on our return and that your safety was paramount.'

'Dear "Uncle" John. It seems extreme but it's possible I suppose.'

Harrison nodded. 'I spoke to the dockside foreman telling him of our damaged tiller chain. He told me two men were looking for work two days ago. Given how busy they are on the docks, he took them on.

'Speaking to him this afternoon, he tells these men have disappeared, didn't even wait to be paid for their time, which in itself is most unusual.'

'A coincidence maybe?' said Beth.

'Possibly, but something or someone caused that bar to be there. The chief engineer tells me he can do a temporary repair but he needs to look at the rudder head and rudder. Due to the water in the docks being so cloudy and dirty, he'll need to send a diver down as soon as we're in clear water to do a full assessment and any repairs before we get into blue water, probably Plymouth.

This will cause a further delay. I regret we'll be here for another few days before the harbour authority can give us a new turnaround date and time. These docks handle hundreds of ships a day, hence the need for the larger Albert Docks,' he said shrugging his broad shoulders. 'Will you stay aboard or return home?'

'I'll stay aboard; I have no wish to add further to your problems, Captain,' Beth said, thinking to herself, so it begins. For she had no doubt it was Feltsham's opening gambit to cause delay, danger and frustration wherever possible. After the meal, which was well cooked, a glass of claret in hand, Beth went to the rail-side gunwale and looked down at the still-busy docks. The new arc lights blazed, lighting up the whole of the Pool of London Docks like a scene from Dante's *Inferno*, she hoped she'd be able to sleep.

At breakfast the following morning, Harrison had some good news: due to a cargo problem on a ship scheduled to leave tomorrow they had been given their slot for departure.

'So we leave soon. I'd appreciate it if you'd address me as captain when the crew are around, for the sake of discipline, but Samuel when we're in private, if that's agreeable to you.'

'Of course it is. I understand completely.'

The day seemed, to Beth at least, to go slowly, but the time came when they were seated once more at the captain's table with a bowl of hot Irish stew. The talk was about their experiences of sheep stations and stories of the sea. An Australian sea shanty drifted in from the forecastle competing with the continued dock sounds. Did they never stop? thought Beth.

If it had been a chaos of noise before, it was as nothing compared with the next day. Shouted orders from the captain, first mate and bosun rang out from early light, ropes wound or unwound, small towing boats moving into position, hatches being battened down, sailors everywhere on the decks into the sail rigging sheets, but finally the anchor was pulled up, covered in the slime of Old Father Thames.

'Away all lines,' came the order and Beth could feel movement under her feet, slow but steady.

They were soon being towed out of harbour on the outgoing tide, into deeper water. The ship moved with the swell, the noise of the docks became less, the wind freshened to a chill and the *Tarn* was free of her imprisoned moorings, sailing into her rightful environment, the open sea.

Beth sighed, she was going home.

A knock on her cabin door brought her back to the moment.

'Come in.'

'Well!' Samuel Harrison said, closing the door behind him. 'We're under way at last.'

'I like a happy ship, Samuel,' Beth said, thinking it was the first time she had used his name. Strangely it came as rather a shock, the intimacy in it, but then it was gone.

'So, with your permission, can we give the crew an extra tot of rum or grog? Once in hand I want to thank them for a job well done. I'll do it from the quarter deck, wishing us all a safe journey.'

Samuel smiled. 'You're the owner, Beth. I your obedient servant and captain; it shall be done.'

With the breeze on her face and in her hair, Beth raised her glass in toast to the cheering and clapping of the crew. On this day, at this time, all was well in the world.

Beth lifted her glass to the sky. 'Shenkin, as God is my judge, we will settle our score with the House of Feltsham once and for all. I'm on my way.'

'Strong words, Lady Standish, but Feltsham lives in a man's world of privilege. His sister will mount a social barrier against you in Sydney and threats will be made against you with attempts to carry them out.'

'Bridges to cross, as they come up. I want to thank you for your understanding about Tinker; he's been with me since I was a child, and with my father before me. I trust him with my life.'

'A formidable character.'

'He is indeed, and a warm caring one too. I cannot think of my life without him. He taught me all I know about the earth, sky, herbs and plants, his language and his spiritual connection with it all. A remarkable man, he cannot understand, for instance, our social culture and it's misrepresentation of our women in it.'

'Captain Saxon told me of your charitable work among the poor and now your involvement with the feminist movement here in London, Beth. You take a lot on.'

'It needs to be done, women are used and abused, with no redress to the law. They are but chattels to an overindulged male-dominated society.'

'Wow! I see why you are one of the cause's leaders.'

'Forgive me, Samuel, but don't get me started on this subject for it is close to my heart.'

'Then let us speak no more about it for the moment. I'll have the steward bring glasses and some Madeira.'

Tinker was returning to his small, but cosy, converted store room cabin.

'Tinker, I was just talking of you to the captain. Will you join us for a moment?'

'I have called for some wine, Tinker. Will you take a glass?'

Tinker gave a shivered look. 'I never touch the European poison, Captain.'

'You see, Samuel, he stays at my side in spite of his condemnation of us.'

'I think you have justly pointed out, Tinker, that we are not so civilised as we would like to think.'

Yes, thought Beth I like this man.

# CHAPTER 14

The following evening while the ship sailed down the Thames then out into the English Channel down towards Plymouth, over their late evening meal, Tinker told them about his people.

'In our society women are respected as both life-givers and the caretakers of life. Which means that they are responsible for the early socialising of the children. The correct term for an Aboriginal is "aborigine", and whether male or female, each have a vital role to play in the wellbeing of the tribe. The men are responsible for providing food, shelter and clothing and we respect women for their spiritual and mental strength. We have been around a long, long time, some fifty thousand years. During that time we developed a thriving society, but European colonisation disrupted and greatly harmed our way of life. They brought guns and diseases. You wanted more and more land which resulted in warfare between us. It ended in the British forcing us from our lands into reservations.

'Our women carried out healing ceremonies and told stories to the children to carry on our traditions. Apart from taking care of the children, our women cook and take on the roles of gatherers. In many cases, they are the primary providers of food because the hunts by the men are not always successful.

'The tools used by the men are mostly made by the women. So you see our women are the roots of our culture; without them we would be lost. Can there be anything more creative than bringing life into the world? That is the sole reason why women are so very important. They are our immortality from generation to generation. You Europeans are so angry at yourselves, at nature and the world around you, which you are determined to control. I tell you now it is a fight you will not win. For every hour you try, you lose sixty seconds of happiness.'

For heartbeats all was silent; only the creaking of the ship and the slow metallic sound of the lamps swinging to and fro above their heads marked the moment.

Captain Samuel Harrison turned to Tinker. 'We have much to learn from the Aboriginals, Tinker, who we thought, and have been told, are violent, primitive and savage and their way of life completely negative. Thank you for correcting that unjustifiable image.'

Beth smiled. 'You see now how much I value Tinker's guidance in life.'

'Indeed I do; it is a lesson for us all. But it's getting late and tomorrow we dock at Plymouth to look at the rudder before the blue water really begins.'

At Plymouth they took on board fresh water and meat. A ships' chandlers provided new tiller pulleys in case they were needed. The sails were reefed in and the ship became becalmed. A diver was sent overboard to examine the rudder unit. By midday, the chief was able to confirm that all was in good order with the tiller, the rudder head and the rudder assembly. They cast off on the outgoing tide and were soon on their way to the Eddystone Rocks and the lighthouse. It would be their last look at Britain for an unknown length of time. Beth felt a strong elation about going back home after, how long was it? Twelve years, at least. For every sea mile that passed under the keel of the *Tarn*, Beth's accent became more and more Australian. Three days later, after crossing the Bay of Biscay, which was no more than a thin faint line of land on the distant shore, the captain informed Beth that they would take on further fresh provisions at the Canaries and spend about five to six hours there.

Late that evening, on the turning tide, Beth heard the captain shout from the quarter deck, 'Mr Billings set a course for Rio de Janeiro, if you please.'

'Sir.'

The evening meal was lamb with mint sauce, new potatoes and broccoli, followed by fresh fruit from the Canaries. The conversation turned to the next leg of the voyage.

'So now we really begin our voyage home. It's some ninety to one hundred days from London to Sydney, so we have a lot of sea miles to cover yet. A long time at sea, Beth. They're saying the Cutty Sark, once it joins the wool trade, could do it in seventy days, which would be a record time. I understand she is capable of doing seventeen knots.' The captain paused for a moment before going on, 'We now face, as you know, from your previous voyages, Beth, the doldrums which is a low pressure area five degrees north to five degrees south of the equator, where the northeast trade winds meet the southeast trade winds cancelling each other out, leaving us with little wind to power our sails. It could delay us by days or even weeks before we pick up the clean trade winds we need, so can I rely on your patience?'

'Need you ask, Captain? We'll be as patient as church mice, shall we not, Tinker?'

'We remember it well, Captain, for we spent ten days in that calm water on our outboard journey to London. There was not even a light breeze. It reminded me of walkabout time, a dream world unfolding slowly. My people have a saying: "Learn from yesterday, live for today, hope for tomorrow".'

Samuel Harrison gave an appreciative smile. 'That certainly covers it, Tinker, so let us hope for the best. Of course, with the coming of steam propulsion this won't be a problem in the future.'

Beth shrugged her shoulders. 'Feltsham is on either the *SS Orient* or the *SS Lusitania* so he'll have no such delay, but it all points to the fact that the BKSS Line needs steamships as soon as we can, Captain Harrison.' Beth said, while the steward began to clear the table.

The following morning, Beth woke to a stillness of the ship that she found unnerving. Dressing quickly, she went to the gunwale outside of her cabin. All was still.

Samuel's voice startled her. 'The doldrums, Beth and only the edge of it I'm afraid. I'll give it to eight bells today, that's late evening, and then I'll decide which way to tack to pick up what wind there may be. By the morning watch, six bells, we'll have a better idea of what we're up against.'

'I'm sure I don't need to tell you how important time is to me, Samuel. Can we row out of this?'

'It may be possible, but how long it'll take to clear us out to the trade winds is a difficult question to answer.'

'I understand.'

'I'll do what I can.'

'Thank you, Samuel.'

By noon the following day, the long boats were being lowered into the water: one on the starboard side and one on the portside, eight men in each. The sun was up, the water calm, their hopes high. The towing ropes took the strain. Steadily the ship began to move, but slowly. The men rowed for two hours then the captain changed crews.

'Bosun! My cabin if you please.'

'Sir.'

'Mr Billings, follow me.'

Once inside the cabin the captain turned to the bosun. 'Do you have a problem, Mr Timms?'

'Yes, sir. I was about to report it to you. It's the halyard, sir. It's been tampered with and the sheets are damaged.'

'So, even if we did get a breeze or a reasonable wind we cannot, at the moment, take advantage of it.'

'No, sir.'

'Sabotage by someone on the ship.'

'Mr Billings, do you have any ideas?'

'No, sir.'

'Bosun, give me a full damage report together with how long it will take to repair.'

'Aye aye, sir.'

'Mr Billing, I want all the crew's paperwork verified and a complete investigation of everyone's movements during eight bells of the last dog watch to eight bells of the morning watch.'

'We have a crew of forty-five all told, sir, it will take a time.'

'Then the sooner you begin the better, Mr Billings.'

'Sir.'

The captain walked to the main cabin and knocked on the door.

'Come in.'

'We have a further problem, Beth.'

'Which is, Samuel?'

He told her of the bosun's findings, and what it meant.

'Damn and blast the bloody man.'

'You believe Feltsham is behind it?'

'Of course, don't you?'

'It appears so. I can repair the damage, but it will take time. I'll also keep the towing going, changing the crews every two hours. I have a top-sail lookout barrelman in the crow's nest to look for any sign of "cat's paws" in the water caused by breezes or stronger winds. In the meantime I'll investigate the incident thoroughly.'

'Let me know as soon as you can.'

'I will.'

The bosun came up to the quarter deck. 'The carpenter's saying it may take two days to repair the damage, sir.'

'Tell him he has twenty-four hours.'

'Sir.'

'How long have we known each other, John?'

'This is my tenth, no twelfth, voyage with you. The first one you were no more than…'

'Go on, no more than a kid who you took under your wing and taught me all you knew about seamanship and much more beside.'

'It was a pleasure, Samuel. I never knew such a youngster so eager to learn.'

'So what do you make of this?'

'I have my forty-five-years-at-sea beady eyes on everything that the crew does, it's someone above suspicion.'

'Me, you, Mr Billings, Lady Standish or the aborigine?' the captain said, adding, 'Unless we find out now who it is, it could be more serious next time.'

'Indeed but remember whoever it is won't risk endangering himself; he's not going to pull out the plug his side of the ship.'

'Let's get to the point of what we're both thinking, John. What do you know about our first mate?'

'His father was a ship's captain out of Sydney. He did many voyages but something went wrong I understand.'

'What and on which ships?'

'Well, that's just it, the main shipping line at the time was jointly owned by Lord Percival Feltsham and Captain Josiah Moxey. I sailed on two of their ships myself on the Tasmanian run. Two months later, the BKSS took them over.'

'So we have a connection. Ask Mr Billings to join us.'

'Sam, take care. This is a serious accusation.'

The captain looked at his bosun.

'My apologies, sir, I'll inform Mr Billings.'

'Thank you, Mr Timms.'

In response to the knock, Captain Samuel Harrison stood up. 'Come.'

Once his visitors were inside he said, 'Gentlemen, thank you for leaving your duties and joining me. Firstly, what have you learned about the crew, Mr Billings?'

'A mixed bunch as you would expect on any ship. All do seem to have had sailing experience of one sort or another, and most are Australians. I have still to go over the ones who are on the long boats, which I'll do when the crews are next changed.'

'It's going to take twenty-five hours or less,' the captain said, looking up at the bosun.

'It now leaves me to go over the paperwork of my officers; I've dealt with Mr Timms, satisfactorily. I'm now going over your paperwork and seaman's logbook. I've asked the Boson to stay because he has some relevant information to add. I hope, given the seriousness of the situation, you will not object.'

'It's irregular, sir, to discuss my background and standing in front of a subordinate, if you allow me to say.'

'Yes indeed, if it's of any consolation, I'm tending my own paperwork and log to Lady Standish. Make no mistake, I am determined to resolve this matter quickly, before something even more serious happens.'

# CHAPTER 15

'How long now, Captain?'

'Every morning you ask me the same question, milord; we are, as you know, on course for Cape Town to take on coal. It's a pity we were unable to go via the Suez on the outward journey and into the Indian Ocean, but we can use it on our homebound voyage, via the Red Sea, so it's the African continent next. The steam-driven engines will make good time to Melbourne, about forty-one days certainly, better than any sailing ship on the old great circle route. Times are changing, Lord Feltsham. Now if you'll excuse me, sir, I have my duties to attend to.'

'Wait a moment, Captain.'

'Lord Feltsham, I must get to my duties, sir.'

This did not stop Feltsham. 'Why can't you increase the speed on these so-called advanced steam-propelled engines?'

'My company, the New Orient Line, forbids me to exceed a specific speed while the new engines are being run in, sir. Now if you'll excuse me.'

Feltsham turned his attention back to his breakfast.

'The salt, Cordelia, for these boiled eggs, and ask the steward for more toast. Talking of toast, your letters should be in Sydney by now should they not?'

'Yes, dear, a week ago possibly.'

'How many will be at the reception?'

'If all accept, then about eighty.'

'It's the governor's wife I want you to cultivate, Cordelia, remember that. I'll see to getting an introduction to the new governor Lord Augustus Loftus. It's a pity we missed his inauguration at the beginning of August; you could have organised something.'

'I cannot think of food, Algernon. I feel so sick all the time. I had a most restless night; I hardly slept.'

'We have yet to go through the roaring forties; the captain says you'll feel far worse when we do. He recommends you get up on deck into the fresh air, not stay in your cabin, which makes the sea sickness worse. But don't trouble me with your malady I have a great deal of planning to do. Ask Bennett to join me on your way to your cabin.'

'Very well,' Cordelia said, getting slowly to her feet.

A little later there was a scuffle at the cabin door.

'Don't just stand there, man, come in.'

The man that entered was Uriah Heep incarnate. Dickens could have based his character from *David Copperfield* on him.

'Good morning, milord, I trust you slept well,' he said, in a dry thin voice

'Yes! Yes! let's get on with it.'

Bennett cringed at the remark. He moved further into the cabin, a stooped figure in black, thin of face, hair and any warmth. On his beaked, sharp, red-tipped nose he wore a pair of pince-nez attached to his coat by a thin gold chain. In fact, everything about him was thin.

'The money transfers should now be complete isn't that right?'

'They should be by now, Lord Feltsham. It's a considerable amount of money, if you'll allow me to say.'

'It will buy my way into the business structure of New South Wales and place me in the position to bring down the BKSS business empire and restore it to my family.'

'The returns will indeed be substantial; their last quote on the London Stock Exchange was staggering,' Bennett said.

'Stolen from me by this scoundrel Shenkin.'

'If you forgive me for saying, sir, it is now considerably more than when Lord Percival owned it.'

'Financed by our money, sir.'

Bennett knew the signs. 'Quite so.' He was an odious little man corrupt enough to accept any, let us say, iniquitous points if it gained him money.

'I need as much time ahead of Beth Shenkin in Sydney as possible: at least two weeks, four would be better. The arranged delays to the *Tarn* should be happening by now. The man was well paid and the threat of his father's crimes coming to light again should secure his efforts.'

After a moment Feltsham continued, 'Are the balance sheets ready for the private bank we intend to open?'

'They are, sir. Two sets of books as per your instruction.'

'Also find me a small newspaper that is in need of capital.'

'But why a newspaper—'

'Don't ask, man, just do it,' Feltsham cut him short.

'Very well, sir.'

'If only this damn ship would go faster, but the captain refuses.'

'The first mate tells me once we take on coal at Cape Town we'll be through the forties in record time and in Melbourne within a very short while, certainly well ahead of the *Tarn*.'

'But I'm in a hurry. Don't they understand I want the trap set by the time the *Tarn* docks in Sydney?'

'Indeed, sir.'

'Let's hope this man our agents have contacted is the man for the job. I'm told he knows a number of what do they call them?' said Feltsham looking through his papers. 'Bushrangers, whatever that is.'

'It refers, sir, to former convicts who escaped into the bush; they rob remote sheep stations or rustle livestock. Our man, one Thomas Travis, is acquainted with one of the most notorious, a so-called bushranger named Ned Kelly. He'll know who to use, to the best effect, in your plans to undermine the BKSS businesses.'

Feltsham's eyes lit up with the expectations of it all. 'Firstly, the sheep stations, by rustling their livestock, then getting diseases into the Home Sheep Station. Then, with the help of our business associates, we undercut their prices on the markets of lamb, mutton, beef, wool and grain.' Feltsham's breathing was coming faster as he warmed to his subject. 'We then target the shipping line; you'll need to place orders for steamships, at least two, for the earliest delivery. Advise the Glasgow shipbuilders we'll pay over the usual cost for a guaranteed fast delivery. Once in place, we'll cut the cargo costs of shipping any cargo anywhere in competition with BKSS's main customers.'

'An ambitious plan, my lord.'

'It's why we're enlisting the participation of other businessmen, so we are not completely risk exposed. In fact by only fifty percent, my dear Bennett.'

Bennett gave a thin-lipped broken-toothed smile, or the best he could do in the way of a smile.

A knock at the cabin door disturbed Feltsham's flow.

'Come in, if you must.'

'The doctor's complements, sir, but can you come to Lady Cordelia's cabin urgently?'

'Can't you see I'm busy?' Feltsham said, irritably.

'The captain is already there, Lord Feltsham.'

Still annoyed, Feltsham entered the cabin without knocking.

'Well what is it?' The pervasive smell of sick was overwhelming.

'Your sister is very ill, Lord Feltsham. She has lost a lot of fluid and is now in a coma,' said the doctor.

'What do you suggest?'

'With your permission, I want to pack her in ice to bring her temperature down. Once in Cape Town she is to be hospitalised for at least two weeks.'

'Most inconvenient for me, in fact impossible; I must go on to Melbourne without delay.'

'You could arrange for her to follow you later.'

The captain turned to Feltsham. 'We have a ship calling at Cape Town about three weeks after us. Your sister could travel up to Melbourne on her.'

'No, but does it go to Sydney?'

'Yes, my lord.'

'Right that's it then. Thank you, gentlemen, now I must get back to my meeting.'

The captain looked at the doctor and shrugged his shoulders as the door to the cabin slammed behind Feltsham.

After more long tiresome days, the *SS Orient* finally docked at Melbourne. Lord Feltsham immediately arranged a meeting of businessmen at his hotel.

'Gentlemen, I am offering you the opportunity to make a great deal of money. I am here to bring down the BKSS by, with your help, first weakening it, then with a hostile takeover. I will put up the majority of the money, supported by five syndicated members, each to receive a percentage cut of the full value of the BKSS business empire.'

The uproar that followed took some time to settle down. When it did, a number of the men had left, most of which had dealt with BKSS in one area or another. The remainder had been in competition with BKSS over many years so the opportunity was compelling. The outcome, once the investment of money was agreed and Feltsham's capital guaranteed, was two percent of the BKSS holdings for each of the five syndicate members. They would undercut BKSS sheep meat prices and cargo charges in the state of Victoria. All investments were to be lodged in Lord Feltsham's new bank with each becoming board members.

After the meeting, Feltsham left for Sydney.

# CHAPTER 16

'The bosun here tells me, Mr Billings, that he knew your father, at least by reputation. A first-class ship's captain by all accounts.'

'He was, Captain Harrison. Then he retired early with sufficient money to buy a fine house, be able to send me to England to be educated and afford me a monthly allowance, we were all surprised by it.'

'He had invested well?'

'So he told us, but it was more money than any investments he could have made on a captain's income.'

'In the meantime you were in England, I see from your papers, and in the Royal Navy, as a midshipman.'

'Yes then I passed my lieutenant exams and was a commissioned officer on the battleship *HMS Resistance*. After two years' service I was called back to Sydney when my father became very ill. I resigned my commission and moved back to Sydney permanently where I turned to a coastal merchant shipping career, mainly between Sydney and Tasmania, which allowed me to take care of my mother and father.'

'Yes, I see it all here in your papers and logbook, but I feel there's more than is written here,' said the captain, putting down the paperwork.

Billings said nothing.

Harrison continued, 'The bosun is here because in his forty years of seamanship he has known many captains and first mates working out of Sydney; he remembers that your father captained a number of the Lord Feltsham and Moxey's ships, is that not so?'

'Yes, but so did many others, Captain Harrison.'

Samuel Harrison noted a fine film of perspiration on Billings's forehead that the overhead swinging lamplight caught.

'That is true, but it's a strange coincidence that Lady Standish is returning to Sydney to refute accusations by the present Lord Feltsham regarding her father.'

For heartbeats all was silent but for the creaking of the lamp and ship's timbers.

'I cannot say more, Captain, please. It is a question of confidences.'

'To who, sir?' Harrison said in a sharp tone. 'While you are under my command, your loyalty is to me and this ship. I demand to know the connection, now.'

At this, Billings took a small Derringer handgun from his boot and pointed it at Harrison.

The bosun went to move forward. Billings swung the pistol in his direction. The captain stood motionless. 'Stand still, Mr Timms.'

He turned to Billings. 'Don't be a bloody fool. What are going to do, and where can you go? We're in the middle of a bloody ocean, man.'

At that moment, Beth come through the cabin door in a rush. She took in the scene quickly, picked up a heavy object from a side table and brought it down on Billings's head with a sickening thud. Billings collapsed in a crumpled heap on the floor.

'You wanted to see me, Lady Standish?' the captain said, with a smile on his face. Adding, 'What did you hit him with?'

Beth looked down at her hand. 'This.'

It was a large hourglass in a solid brass frame.

'That'll do it every time. I've been in a few bar-room brawls but never seen a blow delivered with such accuracy.'

'You're forgetting my father was a bare-knuckle fighter, Captain. He taught me how to protect myself. Is he dead?'

'No, but he's going to have a hell of a headache come morning. Bosun, treat him as best you can then put him in a secure cabin, lock it and bring me the key. No guard, I want this kept quiet. You'll take over as acting first mate. Appoint a leading seaman to assume the position of bosun, both with immediate effect.'

'Aye Aye, sir.'

'Now, Beth, I believe you came to see me about something, is that not so?'

'Indeed I did, we have a breeze which now feels like a wind.'

'I feel it under my feet and hear it in the sails, which must be repaired, give my thanks to the carpenter, and it's a fair wind to Rio, Mr Timms.'

Beth turned to the former bosun. 'Congratulations on your appointment, Mr Timms, and with the captain's permission, perhaps you would join us for dinner tonight?'

'Yes, indeed,' said the captain.

'Delighted, Lady Standish, and thank you, Captain.'

On deck, a smiling helmsman stood firm at the wheel, the wind in his face and billowing sails above him. The longboats were back on deck and being battened down to meet the roaring forties.

'We should, with this wind, be in Rio very soon,' Harrison said, nodding to Beth.

At the captain's table that evening, a light meal was set before them. 'We'll take on provisions at Rio before meeting the might of the roaring forties. I'll sail as close as I dare to the Antarctic ice floods, to pick up the strong trade winds to Australia, and have us in Sydney in a few weeks.'

'Excellent, Samuel, excellent,' said Beth.

'If you don't mind me asking, Tinker, why have you never married, or did you?'

Beth went to explain but Tinker stopped her. 'Thank you, Beth, but it is alright, after all these years the pain is less and I will explain.'

Samuel Harrison spoke in a hushed tone, 'Please, Tinker, I had no intention to intrude upon your privacies.'

Tinker raised his hand. Then, waiting a moment, he lifted his coal-black face to everyone at the table. Beth looked anguished.

'It was why I was in Sydney Cove the night I first meet Shenkin. Merindah, which in my language means "beautiful", and I had been married for only two months. Because she spoke some English she was asked by the tribe's elders to go to Sydney to request we were given a larger hunting ground. Strange, don't you feel, that this was necessary, to ask for land in our own country, but that is another story. Merindah went to Government House but was turned away. I was told later that a well-dressed man approached her asking if he could help in any way. They were seen later at a place of ill repute in the docks area late at night. Merindah had been raped a number of times. The man's description was given to me. A sporting gentleman by the name of Welks of so-called breeding, who owned a pub and brothel; he had two fingers missing on his right hand. I went looking for him that night in every bar along the waterfront. Hearing that a bare-knuckle fight was to take place at a pub on George Street called the Winged Dove, I decided to look there. The fight was between a Jesse Clark and Beth's father, Shenkin. At the ringside I looked up at the fighters. Shenkin had a cut over his eye that was bleeding profusely. Then a man at my side pushed forward. He was counting a wad of money that he had in his hands, but with some difficulty, because two fingers of his right hand were missing.

'I turned to him, he was well dressed and, from the description I had been given, of the right age.'

'"Mr Welks?" I asked.

'His reply was harsh, he wanted to know who I was and what was I doing there. Grabbing my arm he began to push me out. That's when Regan moved forward. Regan was a big crazy Irishman that you didn't argue with; he almost lifted Welks off the ground and told him to leave me alone. Welks broke loose and began to walk away. Shenkin was back in his corner after Clark had dropped to his knee from the last blow, but by now Shenkin could hardly see. His face was covered in blood from the cut eye. I always carried herbs with me to treat stings or cuts, while on walkabout.

'I thanked Regan for his help, and told him to put the herb I gave him onto the cut eyebrow of Shenkin. I then hurried after Welks.

'I found him down near the harbour wall heading for one of the pubs. They say a scream like that of an animal went above the general bawdy sounds of the docks. Someone shouted "Police". In those days Sydney was under military surveillance.

'The fight was over; Shenkin had won. Both he and Regan were walking back to their lodgings. I stood silent in the shadows blending perfectly with the blackness of the night but Shenkin saw me. He always says it was my smile that lit up that dark corner. He said they had been looking for me, that the herb had stopped the bleeding in time for the next round. As we talked, a group of constables and soldiers with an officer came up to me. They began to question me. Shenkin asked the officer what it was about. He was told that they had found a man who had been killed lying up against the harbour wall, that the man had been seen earlier, by a prostitute, being followed by an Aboriginal.

'Shenkin told them it could not have been me then because I had been with them all night, as his cut man in the bare-knuckle fight at the Winged Dove. The officer lifted his lantern. "Shenkin isn't it?" he asked. "Hell of a good fight." Shenkin confirmed it was him, and then asked what had happened to the man.

'The officer grimaced. "Horrific," he said. "The man's genitals had been cut off and stuffed into his mouth, and both wrists were slashed. He died in a lot of pain and loss of blood about twenty minutes ago."

'"Our man here is peace loving, with a black soul it's true, but a heart of pure gold," Shenkin told him.

'"Right," said the officer. He was sorry to have detained us and bid us goodnight.'

Tinker gave a slow lingering whiter-than-white smile.

'And Merindah?' said the captain.

'I took Merindah home. It took weeks for her injuries to heal, but then after two months she began to have sores in her mouth and private parts. She died of syphilis six months later, infected by one of the men who had raped her.'

The captain leaned across to Tinker and placed his hand on his. 'I am so sorry to have raised the point.'

'A long time ago, Captain, she was my morning light, my evening star, the very air I breathed. I was fortunate to have had her with me for those precious few months. I never married again.' After a long pause, he continued, 'That sometime later Shenkin should suffer the same loss due to Lord Percival Feltsham's henchman Ketch brought us even closer together.'

Beth sat perfectly still as the tears run unchecked down her beautiful face.

# CHAPTER 17

The days seemed to speed by. The weather became rougher, and colder. Snow fell as the *Tarn* sailed close to the South Pole causing ice to form on the open decks and gunwales. Soon she caught the strong trade winds and sped her way down to Sydney.

The *Tarn* docked at Port Jackson on a clear sunny morning, a little chilly but fresh and welcoming. A tender took Beth and Tinker to the harbourside where they had a light meal. Captain Harrison had already sent word to the BKSS's home farm to arrange for a carriage to be sent to collect them.

By very late evening, Beth was finally home. George Powell, who Shenkin had given a job to all those years before, now ran BKSS. Rachael, his wife, had given him three healthy children and between them they had built the home farm into the success it now was.

Two men had joined BKSS since Beth had been in London. One was Jake Compton, a very experienced stockman; the other was Paul Garland, an arable land specialist. Both divided their time between all the sheep stations in BKSS holdings.

George Powell advised Beth that he had invited both for a celebration dinner of her return, together with Sir Edward Standish and family.

'Excellent, George, I will join the men after the meal to discuss our present situation and business plans. To this end I want you to invite Captain Saxon and Captain Samuel Harrison, for I have plans for our shipping line.'

George Powell nodded. 'Very well, Beth, I'll send word first thing in the morning, but I should mention to you that Paul Garland is very much a "men run the world of business" kind of man; women do not join the men for port and cigars or give any advice on business.'

'Oh dear! He is in for a surprise isn't he,' Beth said, with a rather acid smile.

George Powell gave a slow smile. 'If you say so, Beth.'

'I do, it's time to bring my thinking and intentions about BKSS's future into focus for everyone, in particular the threat that the present Lord Feltsham poses.'

'But at the moment I want to see Rachael and the children, they must be quite grown up by now, George?'

'They are, Beth. We're very blessed. I know I've said it many times, but we owe it all to your father. I shall be forever in his debt.'

'He always said it's what you do for others that really counts.'

'He did a great deal for so many people, Beth. That this current Lord Feltsham should slander him is a disgrace to his memory and name. We'll fight him with everything we have.'

'Thank you, George. It's why I'm here.'

Beth hugged and cried on the shoulders of everyone that turned up the following evening. She was a little taken back by how old Sir Edward had become and held his hand into dinner. The new members of the staff were introduced to her. She immediately felt a distance between herself and Paul Garland. Perhaps he felt he only had a small part to play in BKSS given that very little produce came from the arable land, since it contributed only a small amount to the overall wealth of the company. She must remember to play that side up in its importance to the overall needs of BKSS.

She was pleased to see Captain Saxon, whose weatherbeaten face had hardly changed.

'Uncle John, would you sit by me?'

'And Uncle Edward on my other side, please. I haven't put place names out, so please sit every other at the table. Rachael can you let them know they can now serve?'

Sir Edward Standish got shakily to his feet. 'I wish to make a toast, so charge your glasses if you would.'

Once ready, Sir Edward turned to Beth. 'My dear, we are all pleased to see you back with us after such a long time in your second home in London, taking care of my son and grandchildren. We know the London office has kept you advised of the business, but we look forward to hearing your thoughts in person.'

Garland snorted.

'Not all I think?' Beth said.

Garland looked up. 'Apologies, pepper I think. Please go on, Sir Edward.'

'I intend to, sir.'

'The toast is to Lady Standish, to our Beth.'

All stood, glasses clinked. 'To Beth.'

The meal passed with talk about what they had all been doing, and then they listened with great interest about the duel between Justin and Algernon Feltsham.

Lady Standish Senior was concerned for her son.

'He is fine, Mama, it was only a flesh wound. He wears it like a trophy of war and a tribute to me. He is as romantic as I am sure Uncle Edward was at that age.'

When the laughter died down and the meal finished, the women, except for Beth, retired to another room.

Garland stood up and called for the servants to serve the brandy and cigars.

Beth also stood. 'Sit down, Mr Garland. We will have both when I say so, but not before.'

Garland looked shocked. 'A little premeditated of me, I agree, but it is the way men do things when they are about to discuss business, madam.'

'Not in my house, at my table, at my expense, sir. However, if you insist, there is, as you know, plenty of room outside.'

'Perhaps we should put it to a vote, madam?'

'Indeed stand up all those who wish to drink and smoke. Those who do will leave the room permanently. Do I make myself clear, gentlemen?' Beth said.

Apart from Garland no one moved.

'A revolt of one, Mr Garland. This is, of course, little to do with drink or cigars, for I have sat through many such moments, but it is everything to do with me running BKSS, is that not so?'

Garland started to speak. 'I...'

Beth cut him short. 'Once in a hole, Mr Garland, you should stop digging. I am terminating your contract with immediate effect on a payment of two months' salary. Captain Harrison, Mr Garland is leaving. Please assist him to his horse and instruct two riders to escort him to the main gate tonight.'

'You have not heard the last of this you... you woman,' Garland said, in a flurry of words.

'At least it will not be at such close quarters, sir.'

Samuel Harrison stood. 'This way, sir.'

Sir Edward noted a slight smile upon the young captain's face as he walked Garland to the door.

Beth resumed her seat. 'Now, gentlemen, to business. I would like a report from everyone at this table on the present state of business of BKSS. Sir Edward, would you start the discussion?'

'Well the bank of New South Wales have only just returned their yearly report on our financial position. George and I went over it in detail and we are in good condition. The balance sheets are in the black so we have robust overdraught facilities, if required. Our debt reduction is steady and in line with our forecast. Therefore, we are in a position to invest in any area you may feel is required to meet Feltsham's threat.'

'Thank you, Sir Edward. George, I take it you concur?'

'I do, we have also bought new machinery to replace some of the old ploughs, much to a number of the old hands' objection, but they are learning to switch the tractors on and off. They'll soon appreciate the difference they make to their workload. Cost sheets are in the monthly report to London.'

'Thank you.'

'Good, progress is essential in this competitive world.

'Mr Compton, as our head stockman, what are your observations?'

'Both the sheep and cattle are in good condition. We have first-class drovers who do not push the livestock too hard and lose fat content as a result. The sheep are large and kept in tip-top condition. However, we have lost some sheep lately to dingoes and Aboriginals, which in itself is not unusual but the numbers appear to be increasing. We've also had a few fires in the bush which can be beneficial at the right time of year, to rejuvenate the land. However, while I support stick fires to improve the land, I feel there's something out of step here.'

'My father didn't object to the Aboriginals taking some sheep; his view was that it was their country and they were entitled to share in its fruits. As for the dingoes, well, they're always with us, are they not?'

'Indeed, Lady Standish, but it seems more than that; it seems organised.'

'Deliberate?'

'Yes, apart from those killed by the dingoes, we've also lost some seventy head of sheep and fifty Holstein Friesian cows.'

'Over all our sheep stations?'

'No, from here at home station.'

'George?'

'Jake's kept me informed of this over the last few weeks. I felt as stockman he should raise it with you at this meeting.'

'What do you suggest?'

'More guards at night here and all our other stations.'

'Sir Edward?'

'I agree. In fact, I would go further; I'd arm them.'

'I agree,' Beth said, adding, 'See to it, George.'

'Right, first thing tomorrow.'

'No, George, tonight.'

'Right.'

'Captain Saxon, how fare our ships?'

'We've placed orders for two auxiliary ships which will take us into the age of steam, much to an old seafarer's sadness. We also have very good men in place to captain them.'

Beth smiled. 'I met one on my voyage home, which is why Captain Harrison is here.'

Beth took a deep breath. 'Uncle John, it's time for you and Uncle Edward to retire,' Beth said, holding both their hands. 'I have spoken to the London office, who are arranging generous golden handshake for you both in acknowledgement of all you have both done over these many years.' Still tapping their hands, Beth went on, 'Please understand, it is time for us to take over.' There was a long pause, and then Beth continued, 'But can we continue to rely upon your good consultations in the future, my dears?'

Both of the elderly men gave a slow understanding nod of their heads.

Sir Edward spoke first, 'We will always be at your service and that of the BKSS.'

'Indeed,' said John Saxon.

'Thank you, both. I had been dreading this moment. You both leave the business in excellent shape and we will endeavour to keep it so.'

'Captain Harrison, you will be appointed to Captain Saxon's role and, George, you to Sir Edward's role with immediate effect.'

'Thank you, Beth. difficult shoes to fill but you have my assurance of my best possible efforts,' George Powell said.

'May I first thank Captain Saxon for his confidence in me, and it will be an honour to serve BKSS, Lady Standish.'

'Not if you refuse to call me Beth.'

The laughter rang around the room, while Beth called for brandy and cigars.

'I have no intention of doing away with all the rituals of you males; I simply intend to join in.'

# CHAPTER 18

'The rustling is on too small a scale, gentlemen. Too small by far, I want them to struggle to get enough head of sheep to market.'

One man stood up, a tall handsome man, very dashing, dressed in a black frock coat with a white shirt and black cravat. He was well groomed with a chin beard and military moustache.

'You pay us cash up front and we get to keep whatever livestock we rustle, sheep, cows, horses, together with whatever else we may happen upon. The rest we slaughter, is that correct?' he said, in a smooth modulated voice.

'It is. May I enquire as to your name, sir?'

'You may enquire by all means. However, it's enough that all the men here know me. It's you who requests our special lucrative services; let us leave it at that, for the moment.'

'As you wish,' Lord Algernon Feltsham said.

'Good my first question is, why?'

'It is enough that my business associates know the answer to that, at the moment.'

'Touché. But since it is the BKSS that you are most determined to weaken, it's rather obvious, is it not, sir?'

'Possibly. However, it is not your concern, sir.'

'I am many things, Lord Feltsham, outlaw, robber, rustler, highwayman and stealer of government gold. But, sir, I do not enter into the personal vendetta of any man for that man's gain. I will have no part in this, sir.'

'Perhaps you should bear in mind that I know where you are tonight, something the police may well be interested in, will they not?'

'If they do, sir, you will not see tomorrow night.'

With that he stood up and walked out. A number of men followed him, leaving Feltsham with a very motley crew and a pale face.

Turning to his agent, Feltsham said, 'Who was that man?'

Coates gave a sickly smile. 'That was Frank Gardiner, one of the leaders of the robbery of a gold escort at Eugowra. A wanted and dangerous man, he is associated with Ned Kelly and his brother. He is not to be trifled with, milord.'

'It seems he wishes nothing to do with us, so let us proceed with what we have,' Lord Feltsham said.

Two weeks later at BKSS home station, Beth asked each member of the meeting for their report.

George Powell opened the proceedings. 'It's serious, Beth. We cannot make our quota to the market. We have lost some two thousand head of sheep and over five hundred cows, all prime stock, and all slaughtered where they stood on the scrubland by sawn-off shot guns; these scatter guns are devastating at short range. Some dead, some dying, very many badly injured, the carcases are rotting in the sun. We're trying to save what we can for our own meat supplies or to go to the Aboriginals. However, none of them are marketable.'

'But why slaughter them?'

'Too many to drive; they'd cover no more than six or seven miles a day. The dust ball and smell would mark where they were for us to catch up with them. They'd never make it off of BKSS property.'

'What about the guards?'

'Were it not for them we would have lost more,' Powell said.

'I'll speak to Augustus Loftus. As governor he should be able to assist; if not then we take a stronger line. The bloody man must realise we're prepared to fight back, vigorously.'

George Powell nodded. 'What are your instructions if he can't, or won't, help?'

'We take it into our own hands, but he must see that Sydney owes a great deal to Shenkin, don't you think?'

'Governors come and go, Beth; they blow with the prevailing wind like all politicians.'

The following week at Government House, Lord Loftus was pleased to receive Beth. He acknowledged all that Shenkin had achieved and done for New South Wales, but apart from a small detachment of twenty men with one officer for two weeks, he felt that trying to guard such a vast acreage was an impossible task. Indeed it was why the bushrangers were able to hide so well in the surrounding outback. He ended by saying he wished he could do more – but regrettably couldn't.

Beth related the meeting to George Powell that night, after being told they had lost another thousand sheep.

Beth took a deep breath. 'So be it, we go it alone. Apart from this detachment, we double our guards.'

'And their orders are?'

'Simple, they shoot to kill; any guard who stops a bushranger is paid a bonus of five pounds at the end of each night. The bodies to be placed at the fences around BKSS, a dead sheep to be placed at their feet. Tinker will show the guards where. Let them rot at the same rate as my livestock.'

'Good God, Beth! It will start a range war. Are you sure this is what you want?'

'Do it, George. I'm protecting my own property. If the governor can't do it, I will. Do it.'

'Very well.'

'And, George, do it now. You're excused from the rest of the meeting.' Without waiting, Beth turned to Samuel Harrison.

'What of the ships, when are they being delivered?'

'Two weeks.'

'That's two weeks too long. Pay a premium if necessary; I want to undercut any cargo delivery prices Feltsham charges to any part of the world. Quote the prices even before the new full steam-powered ships arrive. I also want an advert in the new *Daily Telegraph*. It's to be in big bold print and on the front page. They should jump at it given their competition with the *Morning Herald*. I want a copy in front of me in two days, Captain Harrison. Understood?'

'Right.'


In Sydney, Algernon Feltsham was holding a meeting of his own with a number of Sydneysiders, all businessmen covering a range of enterprises.

'I can assure you, gentlemen, that the BKSS will soon be in difficult financial circumstances.'

A stout man spoke up. 'So you say. But what are your guarantees? For it will take a substantial amount of money, sir.'

Feltsham stood up. He took a leather pouch from inside his frock coat. Untying the lace holding the pouch closed, he poured its contents of gold coins onto the desk in front of them, some five hundred pounds sterling.

'My credentials, gentlemen. There are, of course, more being held here in the bank that I have just opened in Sydney. Members of my syndicate in Melbourne will receive, an already agreed, two percent of the BKSS business. I offer the same too you, is it agreed?' After another two hours it was.

Cordelia had arrived from Cape Town and Feltsham prepared to put into action his three 'S's: Scandal, Sheep, and Social offensive.

'We have the first of your reception tomorrow, Cordelia, do we not?'

'Yes, at the newly opened Royal National Park. Over one hundred have been invited, including the governor who regrettably due to other commitments cannot attend. However, his wife Emma can. I understand they named a town outside Sydney Emmaville after her. Worth remembering when you're in conversation with Lady Loftus.'

'Excellent, my dear, well done.'

'Thank you, Algernon. I will convey more to you when I am able.'

'Plenty to eat and drink, I trust. Do not spare the money; this is our first reception. It will be followed by a grand ball, which my syndicate people will attend. They will spread rumours of BKSS's financial difficulties.'

# CHAPTER 19

'Five dead, two wounded,' George Powell said in answer to Beth's question, adding, 'The detachment officer is not pleased about this and says he will report it to his commanding officer.'

'Really, did he indeed,' Beth said.

'Also that we have placed the bodies outside our fences is a questionable act. That is to say, not on our land.'

'Easily remedied, tie the bodies to our fences, place a plaque above them. It's to read *Beware armed guards patrolling*.'

'But...'

Beth cut him short. 'There are no buts, George, do it. Have the men been paid their bonuses?'

'Yes.'

'Good. Also give two pounds to the men who wounded and captured the others.'

'Beth, you're beginning a dangerous set of rules.'

'I can live with it, George. I mean to send a strong message to Algernon Feltsham. The bloody man will soon realise that I am no mere woman, who can be ordered into another room and taken out only when necessary or worse, sexually needed. I'll see the bastard in hell first, together with his agents and including, if necessary, the governor,' Beth said, in a sweep of sharp biting words.

'I see.'

'Forgive me, George, you have done a great job with BKSS but I am in no mood for lectures, which brings me to the ships. When they arrive, complete with their refrigerated areas, I want guards on them twenty-four hours a day.' Beth turned to Captain Harrison. 'If any damage is done to these ships I will hold you personally responsible, is that understood?'

'I'll try my best.'

'Don't try, Samuel. Do it.'

Addressing all present, she said, 'Make no mistake, my friends, we are in a desperate survival situation. One which I intend to win whatever the cost.'

Sir Edward Standish, who was there in an advisory capacity, looked at Beth, almost, it seemed, for the first time. 'I remember Shenkin saying the identical thing, so many many years ago. Gentlemen, I advise you to carry these orders out to the letter or search for another job.'

'Tinker will your people help? Given what we Europeans have done to them I'll understand if they say no, but would you ask them?' Beth said.

'Of course, this very night.' He stood up and left the room.

'Gentlemen, you will have noticed that a new member has joined our board. Let me introduce you to Mr John Wiseman; he is a financial adviser. No reflection on your or Sir Edward's handling of the money side of BKSS, George, but Mr Wiseman is an international dealer on corporate affairs. We met in London before I left for Sydney. He is completely aware of our situation. My husband, Justin recommended him. Need I say more, Uncle Edward? So please listen carefully to what he is suggesting.'

Wiseman stood up.

He gave a slight cough. He was a small man, neat in his attire, greying hair with sideburns, dressed in black and slightly stooped. 'Gentlemen, Lady Standish asked me to review the financial exposure of BKSS. I can tell you that you are indeed exposed to a hostile bid, as all companies of your size are.

'So how best to counter it? I understand Lord Feltsham has opened a bank in Sydney. I have advised Lady Standish to buy shares in it under a separate company name, the company to be quoted on the London Stock Exchange. BKSS is then to sell one or more of its holdings; this will send a message to Lord Feltsham that Lady Standish is trying to raise capital. He will feel that he has BKSS on the run, after all it is being run by a woman, is it not?' Wiseman put his arms in the air. 'A rhetorical question, gentlemen.

'We lull Feltsham into a state of satisfaction that he is winning. That, in fact, he could well be in a very financially lucrative situation here in Sydney. Our dummy company keeps on buying shares in his bank. Small parcels at first until we are ready to move.' Wiseman looked around the table.

'Any questions?' he said in a matter-of-fact tone. He had obviously done this many times before.

George Powell lifted his hand. 'Will his business syndicate also be fooled?'

'Perhaps not, but his lordship is mixing business with personal anger at Shenkin, who he feels robbed him of his inheritance. I assure you this weakness is a failing we can take advantage of.'

Beth's hand went up.

'Lady Standish, you have a question?'

'Yes, why can't we simple buy out his bank with a hostile bid? The syndicate would realise a quick profit, would they not?'

'Indeed, but you do not want to acquire a bank, rather, you want to acquire Lord Feltsham. That is to say the House of Feltsham, lock, stock and barrel, is that not true?'

'Point taken,' Beth said.

'If we can lure him into such a difficult position that he cannot get out of it, and that loses his syndicated partners money, then they will all dessert him and he will be left vulnerable.

'The shipping line is more straightforward, Lady Standish. If you can afford it, you undercut his cargo prices by a significant amount, one that drives him out of business. Firstly, with two auxiliary ships, part sail part steam for the Sydney–Hobart trade, then the purchase of two fully steam-propelled ships, refrigerated to a high standard and equipped with the latest cargo-handling machinery: both of these ships to make the London markets in record time, one going and one returning non-stop. I will ensure customers in London and America are ready to take full advantage of this. There will be no place for Feltsham to go, but it will be costly, Lady Standish.'

'I understand.'

Beth turned to the board members. 'Gentlemen, I want a vote on this. Do we implement it?'

'Yes,' came a chorus of replies.

'So be it. Please go ahead, Mr Wiseman, and thank you for your report and recommendations. George, see to it that the ships are fully functional as soon as possible. I'll speak to the bank regarding overdrafts, where necessary.'

'Most of it is already in place and I am daily reviewing their progress.'

'Good. Next on the agenda are the sheep stations. First, the home station. Reports, gentlemen, please.'

The first to speak was Jake Compton who confirmed they were continuing to lose livestock, which were either killed or seriously injured. George Powell advised them that he was checking water supplies both for the animals and for their own use in the kitchens; so far none had been tampered with. However, their market shipments were being seriously undermined due to the livestock losses.

Beth nodded. 'Have the government men arrived to support our guards?'

'They have and their officer is outside ready to give his report,' George Powell said.

Lieutenant Thomas Pullman Jackson came sharply to attention at the front of the board members.

'Lieutenant Jackson, ma'am, at your service.'

'Good day, Lieutenant. I trust you had a good journey up to us from Sydney? My apologies for not being able to see you sooner. I await with interest to hear your assessment of the situation.'

'Indeed, ma'am. Firstly, I feel with respect that your actions and instructions to your own guards are extreme, if you permit me to say so, further I...'

Beth cut him short. 'So I understand, Lieutenant, but may I remind you that it is my sheep station, my land and my guards. You, on the other hand, are here to assist not dictate.'

The lieutenant stiffened noticeably. 'I speak as an experienced army officer, ma'am, as to the best way to deploy my men.' His voice had gone just a little shrill. 'I must conduct this operation as I find appropriate.'

'Not on my land and under my command, which is what I agreed with Lord Loftus.'

'Orders from a woman! Out of the question.'

'Lieutenant, you've already made one mistake, now you've made a fatal one. You will, I repeat will, assemble your small detachment, have them mount their horses, then get the hell off of my property.'

Lieutenant Thomas Pullman Jackson stood aghast, red faced and with a look of total disbelief on his face.

After a moment Beth lifted her head from the papers she was reading. 'You still here, Lieutenant?'

# CHAPTER 20

'Gentlemen, I want the guards tripled. George, you will order four hundred man-traps. Tinker you will see to it that they are placed around the boundary of the station without delay. Ten yards off our boundary, with markers to be mounted for our men to be safe outside of the man-trap areas. Livestock to be put into safe scrubland areas. A poster sign to be put up saying, *Beware man-traps in use to cull rabbits.*'

George Powell lifted his arms. 'Beth, some of these traps are now illegal in many Australian states. In fact the last time they were used it was indeed to cull rabbits.'

'Now it will be to cull bushrangers; that's the only difference.'

'There could be an outcry from other sheep stations,' George Powell said in a grim tone.

'I can be extremely deaf when I don't wish to hear, George. Do it.'

'Very well, but I think we may well hear from the Australian Agricultural Company. The AACo can be very strict on this, Beth.'

'I'll cross that bridge when, and if, we come to it,' Beth said, her tone indicated she was not discussing it further.

Three days later, four rustlers had been shot dead, six wounded and five caught in the traps. The word was out. Two things happened in quick succession: the AACo were in touch, asking to see Beth urgently, and the bushrangers had stopped their raids.

Algernon Feltsham sat in a remote farmhouse room the other side of Blacktown. 'Are you telling me that you're not being paid enough or that you're too scared to do the job?'

'Both,' said one of the bushrangers, a man named Andrew George Scott who went by the unlikely name of Captain Moonlite.

Feltsham remarked as much; his agents tried to stop him but it was too late. Scott had Feltsham by the throat in seconds.

While Feltsham was turning red then scarlet, Scott spoke to him in a menacing slow voice, 'Listen, you shitless little man, the risks to my men outweigh the money and I'd be very careful about your remarks, for they may well be your last.' Letting Feltsham go, he stood up, gathered his men to him and left.

Lord Feltsham gasped for air while his agents tried to smooth the moment over. Once done, they advised him Scott would pass the word around. They would certainly get no more help from these bushrangers, never mind how much money was offered. His lordship's main agent, adviser and the man responsible for his safety was Major Ashton, Indian Army retired.

'They have served their purpose, Major, so let us return to the more civilised honest society of Sydney.'

'Indeed, milord, but let us hope they're not all too honest, if our plans are to succeed.'

Both gave a slight knowing laugh.

'I have a reception to attend tomorrow night arranged by my sister Cordelia where we will influence the leading citizens and their wives in our unacceptable plight due to this ex-convict Daniel Shenkin,' Feltsham said, in a still-croaky voice.

'The talk will be all about the Sydney International Exhibition and the gem and mining town Emmaville, so named after Lady Emma Loftus, always good to mention that, milord.'

'I will, Major, I will indeed. We had hoped to hold it at the Garden Palace but given the exhibition it wasn't possible. So it is to be at the newly opened Royal National Park. I expect to see you, Major, in your dress uniform don't you know?'

'Most certainly. My pleasure, milord.'

The following day in Sydney, Feltsham addressed his syndicate members in the office of his small, but to his surprise growing, bank. More shares had been bought both in London and Sydney, in only small batches it was true, but to Feltsham's great delight.

'We are growing, gentlemen; I may make Sydney my permanent home, particularly when we take over BKSS.'

The businessmen from Melbourne and Sydney were beginning to count their profits. They were eager to fund the next step in BKSS's downfall. All were invited to the reception that night and all were charged with spreading the continued rumours of BKSS's financial difficulties.

The evening began well. Feltsham was introduced to Lady Loftus on her arrival. He expressed his pleasure and privilege in so doing. He then complemented her ladyship on her great success in Sydney and that of Lord Loftus.

Her ladyship was a very experienced diplomat's wife; she had heard it all before in most of the capitals of the British Empire, so was ready for what came next.

Lord Feltsham flexed his noble birth. 'I am in Sydney to regain the inheritance stolen from my family by a convict, one Daniel Shenkin. Any assistance would be most helpful, perhaps a mention to the governor?'

'Make an appointment to see him, Lord Feltsham. I never interfere in such things. Ah! There is a dear friend of mine, one of the Dymocks. Their bookselling business is now open. Please excuse me, perhaps we can speak more later.'

Feltsham doubted that. Her ladyship had made it quite clear she would not be promoting his cause, either now or later.

The talk turned to the Sydney Exhibition; it seemed that it was on everyone's lips. Feltsham felt the night was going to be a disaster.

Cordelia assured him she would speak to Lady Loftus again in the evening. In the meantime he must circulate.

'A poor show about one of your main companies, sir.' Feltsham was addressing a rather stout man with a full set of whiskers and a hand wrapped around a glass of strong punch, which seemed a good idea to Algernon given the lack of progress he was making. Once his glass was filled, he returned to the whiskered gentlemen, who had been joined by a man berating him on his drinking.

'It is my liver, sir, I'll do as I wish with it,' he said, in an already slurred voice.

The other man shook his head, then continued, 'I am a Jesuit, sir. Our college St Aloysius is now fully established here in Sydney. We aim to teach our young men the four C's: competence, conscience, compassion and commitment. *Ad Majora Natus.*'

Feltsham winced. 'My Latin is not up to it, I fear.'

'Nor mine,' said the stout gent, who by now needed to sit down.

'"Born for greater things", gentlemen.'

'A noble cause, sir, but will they achieve it?'

'The brightest will, sir, and will show an example to the rest.'

So went the evening, one of meeting the great and the good of Sydney that Feltsham was beginning to realise was not the backwater he had been told to expect back in London. At least they had the opportunity to spread the rumours about BKSS. Whatever he was going to do next must be decisive.

At BKSS George Powell had arranged, together with Captain Samuel Harrison, a meeting with the Rock Davis Shipyard in Brisbane. The meeting was not going well.

'Impossible, my dear sirs, quite impossible. We are at this moment very busy with building the ferries for the Sydney harbour ferry companies, the *Barranjuee* and the *Coomba* are already in service. Several are yet to be built.'

'We require two auxiliary ships within the shortest time possible,' George Powell said.

'Again, it's impossible even for BKSS, who we have done a great deal of business with over the years. You ship our timber to us from Brisbane Water waterways, Blue Gum and Blackbutt all cut from "old growth" forests. Even so, I just do not have the capacity, gentlemen, to build your ships, which can take up to two years to build,' Rock Davis said.

'We're here because we understand you have two ships ready for delivery, is that true?'

'It is.'

For heartbeats no one spoke. 'What if we delivered your timber "free on board", for one year?'

If you could cut the silence before, it was now brittle. Only the sound of the shipyard workers in what was known locally as the 'Big Shed' disturbed the stillness of the office.

Rock Davis sat very, very still while he calculated the risks and advantages. He had been given this unusual name because his parents, while immigrating to New South Wales, were passing the Rock of Gibraltar at the time of his birth. Whether true or not, the silence was now palpable, like a drawn-out knife.

Finally, Davis spoke, 'I do have two ships ready for delivery to a coastal shipping company in Melbourne within one week.'

'Subject to Captain Harrison going over them today we'll take them.'

'I would have to compensate this customer for the delay.'

'We'll underwrite your costs.'

'You'll give me all this in writing?'

'I will.'

Within the two weeks, as promised by Rock Davis, they were delivered to Sydney. Samuel Harrison began the sea trials.

# CHAPTER 21

'Major Ashton has been monitoring the new BKSS ships. Two were delivered to Sydney harbour on yesterday's late tide. They intend to carry out the commissioning and sea trials immediately. The sea trials will be between Sydney and Hobart, they will be, he assures me, accident prone.'

'We do very profitable business on our cargo charges between Sydney and Tasmania, sir. With a great deal of money invested in our auxiliary ships, any loses would not be well received.'

'Quite so and I can assure you, gentlemen, this will not happen,' Feltsham said, adding, 'The major has it all in hand.'

'We do not wish to know the details, only that our investments are protected while we continue our longer term intention of securing BKSS.'

'Indeed, sir, indeed.'

Once they had all left, Feltsham turned to Ashton. 'Find me a ship's captain in Hobart who is prepared, for the right financial compensation, to risk his ship during these trials.'

'One of our ships leaves in the next two hours; I'll be on it.'

'A permanent accident would be the best outcome, Major.'

'Are there any other kind?'

'Good. We understand each other. I look forward to hearing the sad news.'

At that moment Cordelia came into the room. 'I'm running a fever, Algernon, and need to see a doctor.'

Pulling the cord house bell soon had a maid coming into the room. 'You rang, sir?'

'Her ladyship is ailing. Take her to her bedroom, make her as comfortable as possible then call for a doctor.'

By late evening, Cordelia was much worse. The doctor prescribed sedatives, and rest. He believed it was due to the severe sea sickness that had resulted in the coma, and that it had placed a strain on her heart.

'This is all very inconvenient, Doctor. I have most important business here in Sydney, is there nothing you can do?'

The doctor looked up from his writing. 'I'd say it was certainly inconvenient for your sister, sir, since she may not recover.'

'Of course she will; she just tires easily, always been the same.'

'Then she may well have a heart condition and the weakness is now showing up. I feel we should move her to the hospitable for around-the-clock observation.

I'll find a private room for her in the Tarn Wing, which we are very fortunate to have. It was built by a man named Shenkin some time ago in memory of Dr Michael Patrick Tarn, his doctor and friend. But I'm sure you've heard of Daniel Shenkin, here in New South Wales. He also financed the building of the medical school I attended, a remarkable man and generous benefactor to New South Wales.'

His lordship said nothing.

The president of the AACo held Beth in a steady stare. 'It is simply not acceptable, my dear lady, not in any way acceptable.'

'Forgive me; I regret I was not aware of the rules. We will desist immediately. Please convey my apologies to the committee.'

The wind went out of the president's sails. He found himself saying, 'That's very good of you, Lady Standish. I felt sure there must have been a misunderstanding. We appreciate your prompt response.'

'Will you have tea before your long journey back?'

'Decent of you. I will, thank you.'

Beth rang for a servant.

'Tea for two, Alice, if you please, and some of those biscuits I like.'

'Right away, Beth.'

When the door closed behind her, the president remarked, 'The servant calls you by your first name?'

'Indeed! It is my wish, as you must too, my dear sir.'

The president, Mr Charles Penton, was quick to respond, 'Charles, please.'

'Thank you, Charles. Good of you to understand the whims and ideals of a woman. I trust the committee also shares your forward thinking?' Beth paused to take a sip of tea. 'Do they, Charles?'

'Well one or two are still male driven, but were they to meet you I'm confident they would have a change of heart.'

Beth smiled a most beguiling smile. 'Can I test that further, Charles? Do you have a vacant seat on our AACo's committee?'

The president noted the words, 'our AACo's committee'.

'Let me see what can be done. It would certainly be advantageous to have BKSS with us,' he said, returning the smile.

'You are very shrewd, Charles. What you really mean is you'd be able to keep an eye on me, is that not so?'

'I'm sure you would be able to contribute a great deal more than the need for any careful watching.'

They both laughed while selecting one of the freshly cooked biscuits.

As the president rode away, he was not sure who had won. He had come to criticise, but had wound up offering Lady Standish a place on their board.

Beth too was going to Sydney, but by carriage to see the new auxiliary ships. On their arrival, Beth and Tinker found the harbour bustling with activity; after the relative peace of the sheep station it was just a little unnerving. Outside the Fortune of War pub, sailors were already drunk, most of them whalers who had been at sea for many months, so who could deny them some freedom? Nevertheless, Tinker stood between them and Beth. At last they were at the harbourside, the new ships gleaming in the afternoon sunshine. Captain Samuel Harrison called out to her from the quarter deck; the ships were anchored and connected to the outer pier by heavy wet swaying glistening ropes, which beat the water in their efforts to break free.

'I'll send a tender over to you.'

Beth waved back to him.

The small boat came over the side with a crew of two; given the short distance they were soon alongside. Beth stepped carefully into the bobbing sea-sprayed vessel and was rowed out; she had noted the guards on the wharf.

'Good afternoon, Captain Harrison, fine-looking ships. You and George Powell did well to secure them.'

'I hope you'll still feel the same when you see the costs.'

In the captain's cabin, Beth turned to Harrison. 'It's all or nothing, Samuel. These could take Algernon Feltsham out of the shipping business. Tell me about them.'

'Well, as you know, they have the new auxiliary engines, reinforced hulls, schooner rigged, that is to say, she has two tall masts, fore and aft. The tall masts enable us to suspend gaffs, winches, and derricks to be erected for unloading cargo. I'm like a child with a new toy.'

'An expensive toy, Samuel.'

'Indeed.'

'Can I request your permission for something, Captain?'

'Of course, Beth.'

'Can Tinker and I come with you on the sea trials?' What she said surprised her as much as it did Harrison.

'It would be my pleasure, Beth, but it would be a reduced crew; your comfort would not be up to your usual standard, I fear. I will, of course, move out of my cabin.'

The woman in her almost said something she knew she would regret.

'Thank you, Samuel. I think I could cope. After all, I grew up on a sheep station with a father who did not tolerate weak men or women.'

'Right, you'll both need cloths, pea jackets, and rough-weather wet-proof clothing.'

'All ready in the carriage, Captain.'

They both laughed.

'Till dinner then, when I will explain the trials.'

The meal was a basic preparation of meat and vegetables followed by fresh fruit, nothing grand but nourishing enough and homely. When finished, Beth settled back in her chair and gave a small sigh. 'So tell me about the sea trials.'

'Very straightforward really, mainly to ensure the ship can make its particular voyage or voyages safely. That all the equipment on the vessel is in good order, that the crew are trained in the necessary skills and that the sails and riggings are in good working condition. My main concern is with the new "triple-expansion engine", for this we now have an engineer on our crew to carry out his tests on the new-fangled machine. We're being dragged into the twentieth century of steam, Beth; the days of sail are numbered.'

'Indeed, it's why I placed you in charge of the shipping line, Samuel. Now tell me what are the ships' names?'

'Subject to your agreement, I thought this one *Beth* and the other *Elizabeth*.'

'Excellent. I agree. Thank you, Samuel.'

'For the sake of these trials they're already entered in the logs. I'll have them painted on at Hobart.'

'Well, all seems to be in hand, Captain. I thought a walk around the deck for some fresh air before turning in for, what I hope will be, a good night's sleep.'

Tinker said his goodnights and retired.

'I'll join you if I may. I need to check the men on watch, but you'll need to wrap up well; the Tasman Sea is very cold and choppy.'

On deck the night covered them like a wet blanket, as the ship rolled to the movement of the sea. A bright silver moon shone down and danced its light across the waves towards them. Sea spray in her face, her hands tightly gripping the rail, Beth felt the elation of freedom in the wild nature around her. Turning to Samuel Harrison she had to stop herself from falling into his arms. The look on her face said much and he moved towards her.

'Wait! Stop. It's just the night, the moon, the sea. I'm sorry, Samuel. A moment's temptation. It was the woman in me, the passion in me. My failure to control the moment; please forgive me.' She touched his hand as she spoke, which was another mistake. Beth went up on her toes and kissed him while her brain screamed, bloody stupid, bloody hormones, stop now! Beth turned quickly and ran to her cabin, where the scent of him was still in the air.

'What the hell am I doing?' Beth said out loud. 'Now keep calm, girl. Think damn it, think.' Sitting on the edge of the bunk, his bunk, she tried to slow the moment down. Her mind said one thing and her body quite another entirely.

A knock on the cabin door broke the spell.

'Yes! Who is it?'

'Beth, you know who it is.'

'Please leave, Samuel. What happened should not have happened and we both know it, please leave me.'

She heard the sound of him walking down the gangway, the firm positive steps that she was beginning to watch more and more each day.

'What a bloody stupid mess, so stupid. I'm giving out endorphins signs as if they're confetti. Beth my girl, you're walking a very thin line, but worse still my body wishes I had not sent him away.' Again, she said it out loud in short panting breaths. 'Where do you keep the whisky, Samuel my boy, for I am in need of a jolt?'

Beth found it in one of the chart cupboards. Pouring herself three fingers of blended cheap whisky, she drank deep. The burning alcohol hit the back of her throat while her tears hit the front of her eyes. Beth climbed into her bed, doused the lantern, and thanks to the whisky was gratefully asleep before her head hit the pillow.

In the early hours of the morning a thud hit the side of the ship. It was strong enough to tumble Beth out of her bunk and onto the deck of her cabin. The ship had momentarily listed over at a steep angle. Slowly it righted itself, enabling Beth to walk across to her weatherproof clothes. A voice from outside called out.

'Man overboard.'

In the half-light Beth rushed along the gangway to the bridge, where Samuel Harrison was shouting out orders. Tinker moved quickly to her side.

'Get me more light over on the starboard side, sharply now.'

Turning to the first mate, he shouted. 'Damage report, Mr Stevens.'

'Damage to the port bow, sir, hull plates buckled, but above the water line. Running rigging pushed out of line leaving the ship slow to respond to the helm.'

'Are we taking on water?'

'No, sir.'

'Then we go into Hobart under steam only; send the engineer to the bridge.'

'Aye Aye, sir.'

The looming dark shape of the other ship was moving away, but not before Samuel Harrison had had a good look at her with his treasured Porro and Hofmann binoculars, and her captain too, who was standing near the bow directing the assault on the *Beth*.

'Got the bastard!' Harrison said.

Beth was at his side. 'Have we hit something?'

'We've been deliberately rammed by that four-master sailing ship that's receding into the mist off our starboard bow.'

'But a wooden sailing ship?'

'She's iron hulled, Beth, so her superstructure is just as strong as ours. But I got a good look at the captain. I'd remember him again.'

'Are we able to make port?'

'Yes! But more important at the moment is to try to find the man who went overboard. Any sign, Mr Stevens?'

'He could have been knocked unconscious, Captain.'

'Indeed, we'll continue the search.'

'Aye Aye, Captain.'

After twenty minutes or so they saw the man thrashing about on the portside. He sank below the waves as Captain Samuel Harrison dived unto the sea, before coming back to the surface with the man in his arms.

'Get ropes over them,' shouted the first mate.

Ropes made secure, they slowly raised them onto the deck. The man had a bad gash to his head and was unconscious. His arm still around the man, Samuel Harrison staggered to his feet.

Beth threw heavy blankets over them both, then held on to the captain.

'A brave thing to do, Samuel, foolish, but brave.'

'We're all men against the sea, Beth, or I should say all men and one woman. Thank you for the warm blanket.'

'Break open the rum, Samuel. We all are in need of it, but the lookout man to be seen to first.'

'Agreed. Mr Stevens, clear a sick bay area for the man.'

# CHAPTER 22

They finally anchored at Constitution Dock, which was crowded with an array of shipping, including supply ships, and a number of whaling vessels.

Samuel Harrison gave Beth a short history of the famous docks.

'The dock was built and reshaped by convict labour, Beth, using infill rubble and soil from the nearby banks and quarries. The then Governor Denison of Van Diemen's Land completed the work in 1850 and it was opened in December of that year. It was named after the new Australian Constitutions Act of 1850. What was so important was that it allowed the legislative council to create a Constitution which required Royal Assent by Queen Victoria, rather than being signed off by the governor. Things don't move quickly in colonial politics, Beth, so it was not until 1855 that it finally received Royal Assent, some six years after the Constitution Dock was opened. It then became Tasmania.'

'Interesting, Samuel, thank you. Now that we're at the harbour side what are our first moves?'

'The injured man is in the local hospital. I did question him, apparently the ramming ship came out of the morning mist with no lights showing either on the port or starboard side. She was silent and under full sail for maximum impact; it was on us before he could raise the alarm.' Samuel Harrison paused then went on in a resigned attitude.

'I've sent the first mate to see if he can find a damaged ship moored up here that is consistent with the ramming of the *Beth*. I'll also see if we can get repairs done here, and how long it will take. We'll all meet for a meal at the Bird in Hand hotel this evening.'

'Thank you, Samuel. Till tonight then.'

That evening, apart from Tinker who was not allowed in, they were sitting around a well-worn table in the Bird in Hand where they reviewed their findings of the day.

'Not a sign, Captain, of any ship that was recently damaged,' the first mate said in a flat tone, throwing his arms in the air as he spoke.

'Well I didn't think he'd bring it into the main harbour, so it's moored in some bay further down the coast towards Port Arthur.'

'More than likely, sir.'

'I can report that the repairs cannot be done in Hobart. They do not have the iron plates or the means, at present, to fit them.'

Beth arranged food to be sent out to Tinker. Then, with drinks and a meal before them, they each reflected on their options.

In the end Beth said, 'Well, Captain Harrison, the *Beth* is your ship what do you suggest?'

'It's too far to sail to Brisbane for the Rock Davis Shipyard to repair her. I recommend we sail her back to Sydney; it'll be slow but they have the facilities to make her fully seaworthy again.'

'I defer to your experience, Captain, and I see Mr Stevens is also nodding his agreement.'

But Samuel Harrison was staring at a man at the end of the long bar. He was a big tall man, with black hair and a full beard, a vivid scar across his forehead.

'Yes! That's the captain of the ship that rammed us. I'd swear to it.'

At that moment the man turned. Their eyes locked. For heartbeats all was still. The man put down his drink, spilling some over the bar as he did. He began to move quickly towards the door.

Samuel Harrison leaped over the table by the side of them and was at the door before the man.

'We meet again, sir. The last time you were directing your ship into my port bow, is that not so?'

'I don't know what you're talking about. Take your hands off me.'

Another man came up behind Harrison with a knife in his hand and lifted it to stab the captain in the back. It was a short-lived moment. Mr Stevens crashed a chair down over the man's head; the knife dropped to the floor followed by the man who lay in an unconscious heap in the doorway.

The landlord called out to take it outside.

'Good idea,' said Samuel Harrison, dragging the big man through the doorway.

Pressing the man hard up against the outside wall, Harrison demanded to know who hired him to ram the *Beth*.

The man shook his head.

'You'll tell me or I'll beat it out of you,' Samuel Harrison said with a snarl.

Beth stepped forward. 'You did it for money of course, then listen to me; I am the owner of the ship you rammed. Whatever you were paid I'll double it but I will want to know everything, do you understand?'

A glimmer of greed spread across the man's face.

In a slow deliberate voice, he said, 'The money first.' White teeth broke the blackness of his beard.

'Half now, the rest when I believe you.'

'Over a glass of the best whisky they have,' he said in a broad Scottish accent.

'Agreed,' Beth said

'No police.'

'Agreed.'

Drinks were ordered and Beth said she'd pay for any damage done.

'Leave the bottle.'

Beth nodded at the landlord. 'Now let's hear it all from the beginning.'

He first took a deep draught of whisky. 'Two weeks ago, a man I'd had dealings with a few years back approached me with a proposition.'

Beth cut him short. 'What was the man's name?'

After some hesitation and a further drink from his glass, he said, 'One Paul Garland, a miserable bastard, but who had always paid me well for certain things I had arranged in the past for him.'

'So that's where Feltsham got all his information from about BKSS; having sacked him, he went over to Feltsham,' Beth said

'Go on, but first what's your name?'

'I don't think…'

'Don't be stupid, man. We could find you again if we needed too,' Samuel Harrison said.

'Campbell, Angus Campbell.'

'Angus, my name is Beth Shenkin. I own BKSS. You've already cost me a great deal of money, but I need to know who are the men behind this, apart from the one we already know, and I'm prepared to pay handsomely for that information.'

'Better than Garland?'

'Much better.'

'And no police involvement?'

'I've already given you my word on that.'

'The money. I can tell you Garland paid me well.'

'How much did he pay you?'

'Fifty pounds in silver.'

Beth smiled. 'No he didn't, but I will. We all know he could have had it done by someone else for twenty-five.'

Campbell allowed himself a return smile. 'Garland told me to watch out for you.'

'Now, do we have a deal, or do I pass you back to Captain Harrison and his first mate?'

'We have a deal.'

For a moment no one spoke.

Campbell poured himself another three fingers of Glenlivet. 'Garland had another man with him; I don't know his name but he called him the major. He certainly had a military bearing and seemed to be in charge of the proceedings. I was to ram your ship and also the second ship you have on sea trials, which is due in Hobart in three days' time, is it not?'

'Indeed, and you will receive the balance of the money when the *Elizabeth* arrives safely in Hobart, and not before.'

'I think the major has underestimated you, madam.'

'Not only the major, Angus,' Beth said, pouring them all a glass of Glenlivet.

Another bottle was ordered. Placing the bottle on the table the landlord advised them that it was the last of the Glenlivet.

'Then we must make it last for I have something I want you to do, Angus Campbell, so listen carefully. But first a toast,' Beth said, raising her glass. 'I give you confusion to the enemy, gentlemen.'

'At a price,' Campbell said. 'At a price.'

# CHAPTER 23

Lord Algernon Feltsham had his eye on the daughter of one of the most prominent society ladies in Sydney. Lady Edwina Boyd was the wife of the former chairman of the most prodigious bank in New South Wales. Since his death, Lady Boyd had busied herself in the pursuit of social standing. Her daughter Emily was a shy, rather homely girl; she endowed any event with a sombre nervous look that deterred anyone from engaging her in conversation.

Lady Boyd despaired of ever finding her a husband. Then into their social whirl came Lord Feltsham. It was his first social appearance since his sister Cordelia had died, having never coming out of her last coma. Feltsham had considered it a great inconvenience to his social plans, while her doctor had told his lordship that it was certainly inconvenient to his sister.

To remedy the situation, Algernon decided to marry into the upper social structure of Sydney, as early as possible. So the wedding, much to Lady Boyd's delight, was only three weeks later, a grand affair attended by the great and the good of New South Wales.

Emily's dowry bought them a fine house just a few miles to the west of Sydney. Emily displayed all the excitement of a sour apple that had been populated by worms since her birth. However, that was not the point of the plan, which was to secure a place in the minds, if not the hearts, of Sydney society. From this lofty height, Feltsham would pursue his goal to bring down BKSS and claim back his lost inheritance, that the man Shenkin, he would maintain, had swindled his uncle out of.

The news that only one of the new ships that Lady Standish had on sea trials had been damaged was indeed bad news considering the cost he had gone too.

A meeting was arranged to speak to the major as early as possible.

In the meantime, a wedding reception was to be held that evening in their new lavish home. The carriages rolled up to the front gates in what seemed an endless procession of horses' hoofs. Emily was dressed in an over-flowered dress of blue and red, which did not match any part of her colouring. Her hair was piled upon her head precipitously; in comparison, the Leaning Tower of Pisa seemed more upright and safe. Feltsham distanced himself from the tottering sad figure of the now Lady Feltsham. On the other hand, Lady Boyd filled the role of hostess admirably, leaving him finally to have the ear of the governor and the leading judges of the colony. He felt ready to press home his case for justice to be done against BKSS and to restore their assets to their rightful owners.

Major Charles Ashton explained that the reason the second ship was still seaworthy was due to poor weather conditions that morning. However, the man he had employed to ram the ship assured him he could get two men on board this vessel once she was moored at the dockside. They would damage the rudder, the auxiliary steam engine and the running rigging. The ship would have no driving power and so be unable to carry cargo anywhere. 'In the meantime your syndicate's ships, which are busy with their own cargoes, will also be offered BKSS's cargoes.'

'Good work, Major. This will cripple their shipping business. I want you to be at Hobart to direct the operations from the quayside at Constitution Dock. I understand the ships are to be named *Beth* and *Elizabeth* is that so?'

'It is, Lord Feltsham.'

'How very touching,' Feltsham said.

'I'll leave for Hobart tonight to make contact with the captain of the ramming ship, one Angus Campbell.'

'No names, Major. That's your side of our arrangement. I do not want anything traced back to me, is that understood?'

'Yes, of course, forgive me.'

'Now I must return to my guests, leave by the back exit and I look forward to hearing the sad news regarding the *Elizabeth*.'

Beth gave a slow tolerable smile. 'You understand what I am saying, Angus, don't you?'

'I do.' Angus paused. 'But to work with the police here in Hobart, what will my men think?'

'I'm paying you handsomely to do it. From which they will also benefit will they not?'

'Well some of them. Just the three we'll put onboard the *Elizabeth*.'

'Angus, you are a rogue. What did you do before you came to Van Diemen's Land? Although I should say Tasmania now.'

'I was a school teacher in Scotland, which I found very unprofitable, so I robbed a bank. The judge gave me twenty years' hard labour to be served here in the colonies of Australia. I taught the commandant of the prison's children

Latin and mathematics; he was so pleased he arranged my early release. I seized the day *carpe diem*, as Horace put it, and I never regretted it.'

Captain Samuel Harrison shook his head. But Beth still smiled. 'Do you know, Angus, I am beginning to like you,' she said.

Samuel gave her a look of utter amazement.

'I know, Samuel. He rammed the ship that you were the captain of and you know he is for sale to the highest bidder, that he is a rogue and I know it but the thing is he knows it. There is a certain truth in that, that we can use.'

'You can indeed for the right price,' said Angus Campbell.

'You see what I mean?' Beth said.

'But the man's a rogue, an out-and-out scoundrel.'

'We fight fire with fire, Samuel; we need a good scoundrel on our side. Think, man! Feltsham won't be expecting it.'

'But…'

'There are no buts, Samuel. It's what I intend to do.'

Angus Campbell sat and smiled then turned to Beth. 'My dear Lady Standish, should you ever consider becoming a, shall we say, disreputable lady, I would be only too pleased if you would join us.'

'Praise indeed, Angus, I have a feeling I may just have done so.'

'Then we are in agreement. I offer you my services, for the right price, to arrange a profitable double-cross of the major.'

'Good. But first you will come with me to the Municipal City Police Force here in Hobart, which by a strange coincidence is on Campbell Street.'

The smile drained from Angus Campbell's face.

# CHAPTER 24

In 1804 with the settlements of Hobart Town and Port Dalrymple already established it became necessary to form a police protection group. The then Lt Governor Collins had only a small pool of labour to call upon, so he decided to staff the force with convicts, to maintain order from dawn to dusk.

This was not a great success; crimes were not being reported due to the fear of reprisals from their fellow convicts. By 1806 Collins replaced the convicts with armed military patrols, but the convicts became bushrangers and continued to raid sheep stations out in the bush areas. Soon crime was becoming a drawback in the development of the economy.

In desperation, Lt Governor Davey imposed martial law and Governor Sorell appointed more district constables, but with the arrival of more convicts, bushrangers continued to increase robbery, fraud and sheep stealing at an alarming rate. By 1818 settlers did not feel protected by the small, mostly convict-staffed police force.

When Lt Governor Arthur took office in 1823, one of the first things he did was to reorganise the convict system by strengthening and centralising the police force. Finally, a fully armed field police began to deal effectively with bushrangers. Arthur was a very experienced administrator and by 1828 he had established nine police districts, each controlled by a magistrate, under a chief of police in Hobart Town. While some corruption was still rife, on the whole, property and persons were more secure. The main problem was the continued arrival of yet more convicts with many going to the notorious penal colony at Port Arthur. Arthur had selected the site in 1830 due to its location on the Tasman Peninsula, which was surrounded on three sides by shark-infested water. It formed a natural prison from which few escaped, thus stopping the increasing number of convicts joining up with bushrangers. Some fourteen thousand prisoners were held there at one time or another, few survived the brutality of their sentence and are buried on the 'Isle of the Dead' in unmarked graves.

The campaign against the Aboriginal Tasmanians, known as the Black War, occurred during his term of office. He forced the Aboriginals into reservations and virtually declared an 'open season' on the indigenous people during the war. Many Aboriginals died or were subjected to the law of being reported to the police for hunting for food for their tribes, being near any European settlements, or simply being seen on the streets of a town. Arthur decided to segregate the Aboriginal people on the south-eastern peninsula of the island. Several thousand armed settlers, backed by the British military, were formed into a black line to drive the Aboriginal people out of the bush. Finally, they were settled on the Bass Strait island of Flinders, but by now they numbered no more than two hundred; on Flinders Island their number dwindled even further, they were becoming extinct in their own country.

Governor Arthur did bring about economic development and some law and order, mostly in favour of the European settlers who took over prime fertile areas of Aboriginal hunting grounds and living areas for their farming and sheep stations. By 1866 there were twenty-one municipal councils and eight police districts controlled by the councils or by appointed inspectors of police.

However, the Launceston riots, as recent as 1870, found the police wanting and magistrates were fighting to hold on to their criticised police forces.

Into this troubled past of social unrest strode Beth Shenkin, armed with steely determination, bloody-mindedness and an unshakeable belief in her father's reputation and continued good works, and one named William H. Tobias Hobart's magistrate of police.

Samuel Harrison sent a message to the council requesting a meeting with Councillor Tobias for Lady Standish. Within an hour a reply was sent to the ship.

Magistrate Tobias would be delighted to meet her ladyship, that very afternoon if that was convenient, he would send a carriage and an escort to attend her ladyship. He regretted that he was not able to see her that morning due to council business.

The chairman of the municipal council sat in the middle of the top table in the rather austere surroundings of their offices on Campbell Street.

'Gentlemen, we are brought together to discuss the final details of the installation of our new superintendent of police this coming Saturday.'

The chairman was round of face, plump of body, but nevertheless shrewd of mind. Unlike most of the colonial appointments, he had achieved his social status by developing the economy of Hobart and Tasmania in general. He owned a number of taverns, shops and a thriving ships' chandlers store on the wharf of Constitution Docks. It had once belonged to Captain Josiah Moxey, who had captained the convict ship that brought Beth's father, Daniel

Shenkin, to Sydney to serve his sentence. Many years later her father sold, at below market value, the business to a grateful William H. Tobias for his help in providing him clothes to replace the convict garb he wore following his escape from Port Arthur Penal Colony; it set William Tobias on a successful business career, he never forgot it.

# CHAPTER 25

Councillor Tobias waddled rather than walked over to the door of his office to greet Beth.

'You do us a great honour, Lady Standish, please take a seat. Can I offer you some refreshment, a cup of tea perhaps?'

'No thank you, Councillor Tobias, but I do need your help in a certain matter.'

'We are at your disposal, your ladyship.'

'It's regarding my ship the *Elizabeth*.' Beth paused for a moment. 'Someone is intending to sabotage her in two nights' time.' It was a blunt statement that brought Tobias up sharp.

'You know this in advance?'

'I do, and it is why I'm here.'

'Please go on.'

'It will be attempted by three or four men; they'll have a leader who goes by the name of the major. I don't know his full name, but he'll organise the whole affair to cripple my ship.'

'I see. How can I help?'

'I want a cordon of police around the ship, arrests made and statements taken that identify the man responsible for the attempt.'

'And your suspicions are?'

'Someone who wishes to put me out of business.'

'Here in Tasmania?'

'Yes, and in New South Wales, together with many other places in the world.'

'Forgive me, your ladyship, but your business is?'

'I own BKSS.'

To say Councillor Tobias was startled would be an understatement. The jovial round face became set in a more deferential mode; serious in the extreme might have just covered it.

'But that is Daniel Shenkin's business, a man I greatly admire and one that I owe much too.'

'I am his daughter, Beth Shenkin. My father died a few months ago back in his beloved country, old South Wales.'

'I didn't know, my deepest condolences Lady Standish.'

'Beth, please.'

A light came into the magistrate's face. 'Standish! Of course, Sir Edward Standish assisted in your father's escape from the Port Arthur Penal Settlement.'

'Indeed, and I married his son Sir Justin Standish.'

'I remember the other man was an Aboriginal, who I refused to allow into my clothing shop at Risdon Cove on the east bank of the Derwent River.'

'Yes! Tinker, he stands outside at this very moment, still not allowed to enter any European establishment. Without him the escape would have failed and you would not be where you are now.'

William H. Tobias called for his clerk.

'You called, sir?'

'You'll find an elderly Aboriginal outside on the road; muster as much respect as you can and ask him if he would be good enough to come into my office.'

'But he's an Abo, sir I...'

'Do it, John. I have my reasons.'

'Very well, sir.'

Tinker's black smiling face and white cotton hair nodded at the magistrate with the easy dignity that he always carried.

To his credit, William Tobias stood up and offered Tinker his hand. 'I owe you an apology, sir, for my behaviour so many years ago. Please take a seat.'

Beth thanked him. 'I'm most grateful for your appreciation of the facts, Councillor Tobias. We all owe Tinker a great deal.'

Tinker's smile widened. 'I'm glad to see that the Europeans are beginning to become civilised at last, or at least some of them.'

They all gave way to laughter that eased the tensions of the moment.

'Now what is the plan you have in mind, Beth?'

'We close the door behind the men attempting to cripple the ship with your cordon of police force on Constitution Dock.'

'Agreed.'

'My Captain Samuel Harrison alerts the night watch to feign sleep while the saboteurs get aboard.'

'Understood.'

'You arrest the gang and the so-called major, together with the leader of the gang.'

'And he is?'

'A name you may be familiar with, Angus Campbell.'

'Why! We've been trying to catch this man red-handed for years. I'm most grateful to you, Beth.'

'You may not be when you hear what I have in mind.'

'Which is?'

'Let us wait until your officers have arrested the perpetrators of this attempted crime.'

Magistrate Tobias began to say something, but Beth put her hand up. 'Please trust me, William, in the good name of my father and his generosity to you so many years ago.'

'Very well, Beth, but I hope I won't regret it; the costs of an operation of this kind will be expensive to the police purse here in Hobart.'

Beth nodded. 'I undertake to cover all the costs by a donation to the future development of the police force in Hobart and any possible damages to the docks during the operation.'

'Well that reassures me for I am answerable to the council for all financial spending.'

'Of course, I understand.'

'I need to know the day and time this is due to happen. We have a new Inspector of Police being appointed this coming week, so I hope it's within the next few days.'

'It's in two days' time at 3am.'

'Very well, that's agreeable; I'll have an officer at your side to protect you.'

'Not necessary, Tinker will be my constant shadow as always.'

'But we cannot arm an Aboriginal; I am sorry Tinker.'

'It is of no consequence. I have my own ways,' Tinker said, the bright white smile still in place.

'Right,' Tobias said, just a little apprehensively, 'we'll all meet at the Bird in Hand at 1am. I'll deploy my men; you'll ensure Captain Harrison has the night watch in place onboard ship.'

Beth stood up. 'We are agreed, and I thank you again for your assistance.'

Councillor Tobias put out his hand. 'This maybe my last act as the Hobart magistrate, Beth, for moves are afoot to relinquish our control of the police in favour of a Tasmania-wide organisation under a police commissioner who will report to a democratically elected parliament. It will at least give me the opportunity to repay my debt to your father and that pleases me.'

'Thank you, William, for I have a greater justice that needs to be met.'

'I look forward to hearing about it. In the meantime, I trust you with my own reputation and that of the Hobart Police Force.'

'I'll not fail you, William, is that not true Tinker?'

'If you say, *so it shall be.*'

Two nights later, under a full moon full of bright stars that fought for the right to be seen in the heavens' darkness, it became cold and they were soon all well rugged up. Three carriages of police and former convicts led by Magistrate Tobias clattered out of the rattlers and made their way to the Bird in Hand.

All said their good mornings and Captain Harrison confirmed the ship was in a state of readiness.

'Then let us proceed,' Magistrate Tobias said from beneath a multilayer of top coat and scarves. He resembled an overweight penguin and walked with much the same gait, slow but with intent.

Samuel Harrison looked at his hunter pocket watch again. 'Half an hour to go,' he announced.

'Stay close to me Beth,' said Tinker. In his hand he held a curved stick that the Europeans call a boomerang. Made of mulga wood, Beth had seen Tinker kill many rabbits with it to go into the pot during walkabout times.

'I will, Tinker.' However, Beth also removed a Derringer.357 COP handgun from under her skirt which she always carried, as her father said being prepared is better than being unprepared.

The Derringer handgun is a single-shot, rifled-bored, close-range pistol, so bad breath distance would be its most effective range. Utterly safe to carry, quick to employ and devastating at this close range, a perfect woman's handgun with a smooth polished stock, short, light and easily concealed in a purse or stocking top.

'We will wait for the saboteurs to arrive and get their men on the ship. We will then close the cordon of police constables behind them and secure the area,' Tobias said.

After some time discussing the last details of their plan, Captain Harrison looked at his hunter pocket watch again. 'Get ready.'

'Stay close to me,' Beth said to Tinker. Despite the many times she had seen his skills with his boomerang, she gripped the smooth comforting stock of the Derringer, which was now in her hand.

Four men came out of the darkness and slowly made their way onto the ship; all carried iron bars. Once onboard, William Tobias called out, 'Now!'

Lanterns came on in a semi-circle around the *Elizabeth*.

One man came running down the gangway. Beth, gun in hand, stood in his way at the bottom. The man pulled a knife from his belt. He was within a yard of Beth.

There was a *swish, swish, swish* in the air and the man fell at Beth's feet, blood streaming down his face from a deep gash to his head. Beth looked over to Tinker, boomerang back in his hand, the elbow of the boomerang standing proud, knife edge covered in blood. Smiling, Tinker said, 'One for the pot I think.'

Covering the other three men with her Derringer, Beth marshalled them over to the warehouse area where the major and Angus Campbell were already handcuffed.

Later, they were all gathered at the magistrate's office, where the interrogations had begun.

The major stood up. 'I demand to see a representative from the British Embassy for legal presence. I was taking an innocent walk on the docks, due to insomnia, when I came across these ruffians. I have nothing whatsoever to do with these events.'

Magistrate Tobias looked up. 'Sit down, Major Ashton.'

The silence in the room was palpable. For heartbeats no one spoke.

Tobias opened the file in front of him. 'It is Major Charles Ashton, Indian Army retired, is it not?'

'How...'

The magistrate put his hand up. 'We sent your description, which your co-conspirator Mr Campbell gave us, via the new overland telegraph line to the army both in London and India. The OTL service is in its early stages but functional nevertheless, which is most fortunate for us, but very unfortunate for you. This is the 1870s, Major Ashton the world is getting smaller, too small for anyone to hide in. We are fast approaching the twentieth century, Major; Kookaburras now sit on the telegraph wire. The file that arrived during the night confirms your identity and gives your name rank and army record. It states this officer was facing a possible court martial regarding mess funds in Bombay and Madras. Food was also stolen and sold on the black market at high prices during the famines in Madras. Before the court martial was convened, you resigned your commission and made your way to a remote part of the world at the time, Sydney. With no pension you sold your military training to the highest bidder. We want to know who this man is, in a statement signed by you.'

'And if I refuse?'

William H Tobias shrugged his shoulders. 'I would not advise it, Major. Port Arthur Penal Settlement was closed eighteen months ago. However, we have retained a few cells for difficult prisoners. Most of them are occupied by rats and the place is serviced by only a few guards: one a week I understand. Given your involvement in the crime of attempting to cripple a ship owned by the BKSS Company here in Tasmania, I'm confident I could place you in Port Arthur for the next ten years. In fact, both of you,' said the magistrate looking at Angus Campbell, who turned to Beth.

'Wait! Campbell, wait,' Beth said.

'You'd never get away with it, where's your proof in our involvement?' Ashton said.

'Try me. I don't know what Lady Standish has in mind, but I am the magistrate of police here in Hobart. You have both cost my department, and labour forces, a great deal of time and money and me a night's sleep. So what is it to be, statements and a local prison? Or Port Arthur and the sharp toothed rats? Your choice.'

The file on the desk was joined by another file brought in by the clerk. Standing, Beth was able to read the front of the file upside down.

*Lord Percival Hugo Feltsham: Deceased*

This is no backwater, thought Beth; William H Tobias is a clever man for a former clothing shop owner. He's not going be pleased when he knows my intent.

For heartbeats only the sounds of the early morning chirping of birds, the background of the ocean and the sunshine breaking through the window blinds disturbed the moment.

# CHAPTER 26

Major Charles Ashton, Indian Army, retired, shifted uncomfortably in his chair. Finally, he straightened up. 'How long in the local prison?'

'Three years maybe four.'

'I want to make a deal.'

'That is the deal: Port Arthur or the jail here in Hobart.'

Beth moved forward. 'With your permission, Magistrate Tobias, can we hear what Major Ashton has in mind?'

Grudgingly, the magistrate agreed.

Ashton took a deep breath. 'I'll name the man behind this, his intention to take over BKSS, his syndicate members from Melbourne by name, his fraudulent capital in his Sydney bank, his hiring of bushrangers to rustle sheep from BKSS, his ramming of the *Beth* and tonight's attempt on the crippling of the *Elizabeth*. Once the weakening of BKSS was complete, he was going to make a hostile bid to take over the company and regain his believed lost inheritance, by naming Shenkin as the man that robbed his uncle out of all his assets in Australia.'

Beth sighed. 'It's everything I want in a written signed statement. Will you do the same as confirmation of what you know of the major's statement, Campbell?'

Campbell didn't hesitate. 'Yes.'

'And in return for this?' the magistrate said.

'Safe conduct out of Tasmania,' Ashton said.

'Impossible,' Tobias said, slamming the files down on the table. Dust floated up, glittering in the bright morning sunshine.

'I'm sorry, Councillor Tobias, but this is what I need for a greater justice.'

'They're both going to Port Arthur, Lady Standish, for a very long time.'

Beth noted the use of the title.

'I am determined that my father's, and I might add your benefactor's, name and reputation is kept intact and his legacy to protect the underprivileged in society continues. To that end, if these statements are so written, naming the man responsible, then I will not press charges.'

'You have no jurisdiction in the matter. The crime was perpetrated here in Tasmania of which I am the magistrate of the police force that enforced the arrests.'

'If necessary, I'll put, in writing, that I allowed the men to come aboard my ship tonight,' Beth said.

'Damn it, woman, you cannot do that; to lie about this serious crime would mean that you are an accessory.'

'Prove it, and do not woman me, sir. I am not a second-class citizen. My company, my ship, my decision. Make no mistake, I will do whatever is necessary.'

Dust settled, as silence prevailed in the small office while the magistrate considered his options and his long-overdue debt to Daniel Shenkin. Very soon there would be a centralised administration for the police in Tasmania and his department would be discontinued. This was his last chance to fulfil his debt to Shenkin.

'Clerk.'

The clerk came into the office, writing pad in hand. William H Tobias allowed himself a small smile. 'You are prepared I see, John.'

'Sir.'

'Right, Major Ashton, you first. Begin.'

It took over two hours to complete, agree and sign the statements. When done, the magistrate gave copies to Beth. 'I, of course, suspected Feltsham given the file on his uncle, Lord Percival. So I trust you're satisfied, Beth. Is there anything else I can do for you?'

'No, and thank you again for your understanding.'

Turning to the major and Campbell, he said, 'Campbell, if I see or hear of you again on Tasmania you will indeed go Port Arthur. Now get out of here. Guard, remove the handcuffs. Major Ashton, your papers please.'

Ashton looked bewildered. 'Papers?'

'Army dishonourable discharge papers, freedom of passage, or some form of identity.'

'No, but you have my file there in front of you.'

'I need verification, just a routine matter for the file you understand.'

'No nothing.'

'I see. Then you are on a vagrancy charge. That's a three to six months sentence, possibly a year given your resistance to arrest. A word with the judge I think. Sergeant, take him down.'

Shouting and screaming, Major Ashton, Indian Army, retired, was removed from the office.

'You're a hard man, William.'

'I will have my pound of flesh given a night's loss of sleep.'

The following morning, Captain Samuel Harrison and Tinker stood waiting at the gangway up to the *Elizabeth*. 'Are we ready to set sail for Sydney, Captain?'

# CHAPTER 27

In Sydney, Beth was told the sad news of Sir Edward's death and that her husband Justin was on his way to Australia. Sir Edward had elected to have his ashes scattered over BKSS land. The funeral was attended by Lady Standish senior, Captain John Saxon, George Powell and his wife Rachael, together with all the staff of the home farm.

Tinker rejoiced that his friend was on the great walkabout and had gone back to the dust and the wind that would whirl around them forever. The rest cried.

Having held it together for so long at the sight of Justin, she fell sobbing into his arms at the quayside on his arrival in Sydney.

'Next to my father, he was BKSS, Justin.'

'I know, I know. Did the funeral go as well as can be expected?'

'Yes, but Uncle John was very upset and his sea-weathered face from all the years at sea is now that of an old man. Your mother is inconsolable and just wants to return to their London home. Dear God, Justin they're all leaving us.'

'Tinker would say it's as natural as night follows day.'

'Indeed, he was the only one who could not understand our grief. On top of it all, that man Feltsham and his syndicate have made a last-minute hostile bid to take over BKSS. Even in the face of all the statements I wrote to you about, he could still do great harm to BKSS, the bloody, bloody man. I will see his end if it takes my last breath to do it. I'm holding a board meeting tomorrow and, as a non-executive director, will you please attend, Justin?'

'Yes, of course, but I must spend time with my mother and Jenny, my aunt, and there are the arrangements to be made for our return to England.'

'Of course. Samuel Harrison, who will captain the ship, is preparing the *Elizabeth* over the coming weeks and also seeing to the repair work on the bow plates of the *Beth*. He advises me that the work is going well. I also need at least a few weeks, my dear, to open the Charity Foundation Home here in Sydney, which is a fine building just off Macquarie Street and not far from the old convict barracks that Shenkin was first sent to when he arrived in Sydney to serve his sentence. Like the barracks, it was designed by the convict architect Francis Greenway, convicted for forgery in 1814 and given a fourteen-year sentence. His collaboration with Governor Macquarie resulted in many fine buildings of which this is one. These days the courts and legal administration buildings appear to cover most of the area and the hospital is there of course. But it will be good to see the Foundation opened and the first needy people admitted. Also, my dear, the news that you brought with you from London tells me that Florrie has also found a house in Regents Park for the London Foundation Centre, some thirty rooms in total, which is perfect. I'll send her a letter of credit to buy the property or secure a long-term lease, whichever the owners are asking for. It's in safe hands with Florrie dealing with it, and a great help to me while I am defending Shenkin's reputation and legacy here in Sydney. She also says that Maria Alvarez is filing papers of bigamy on behalf of her sister against Algernon Feltsham.'

The following evening all the board of BKSS were seated in the main room of home farm. Beth stood up. 'Gentlemen we are here to discuss the hostile bid by Feltsham's syndicate. BKSS is the target company they wish to take over without the consent or approval of the target company's board of directors. In other words, the target company's management, that is to say us, are not in favour of the takeover, hence the word hostile. Do I understand it correctly Mr Wiseman?'

'You do indeed, Lady Standish, and as your financial adviser I feel the time has arrived to take the necessary precautions to vigorously fight off this bid. Firstly, the syndicate can go directly to the shareholders and offer a tender bid to buy their shares at a premium price without having to go through its board of directors, or even by trying to replace the target company's management.'

At this Wiseman looked at each man at the table.

Beth spoke straight away, 'I vouch for every man here, Mr Wiseman.'

'Good, no back door open then. So we now consider all the shareholders who may be tempted by a premium price offer.'

Again Beth spoke, 'The main shareholders are sitting at this table, Mr Wiseman, and, as you are aware, I am the majority shareholder, and mine are voting shares, which gives me control of over fifty percent of the company and any vote on this board.'

Wiseman allowed himself a smile. 'Then I declare the company is self-contained. We now look at the shares or stock we have acquired in Feltsham's bank, purchased by a number of private individuals both in small and large amounts of shares. The success of the bank encouraged Feltsham's syndicate to invest more and raise the necessary capital to launch this hostile bid.'

Wiseman, with a gleam in his eyes, also stood up. 'We sell our shares in his bank, gentlemen, all of them. He'll be undercapitalised both in his bank and in this hostile bid. We spread the news to create a run on the bank by its depositors who will remove their funds. This will also alarm the Feltsham syndicate members, who will also remove their holdings.'

'Good God! He'll be left with nothing here in Sydney, absolutely nothing,' Beth said, slowly taking her seat at the head of the boardroom table.

'That's what you hired me for, Lady Standish, was it not?'

# CHAPTER 28

Word was leaked to the *Sydney Morning Herald*, and an editorial was written regarding the financial problems of Feltsham's bank. The run on the bank was immediate; within three days it was closed and an enquiry was set up to investigate the collapse, and Lord Feltsham's part in the closure.

Seated at a long table at the top end of the courtroom were the governing bodies of Sydney's regulating authorities. In the centre sat Lord Augustus William Fredrick Spencer Loftus who had been appointed governor of Sydney only that year after many diplomatic positions around the world. While he was an experienced administrator and diplomat, he knew nothing of colonies and parliamentary government having spent much of his career in Europe, both in British legation roles and at several European courts. At that moment he was the 'toast of the town', with the papers expressing the honour that had been placed on the colony by appointing such an eminent peer as their governor, and they forecast a bright future for New South Wales under his governorship. What he lacked in knowledge about the workings of the colonies he made up for in his expertise in tact, persuasion and administrative adroitness.

'Please take a seat, Lord Feltsham. This shouldn't take long.'

Algernon Hugo Feltsham sat while slowly removing his kid gloves.

'Before we begin, and for the record, would you appreciate a reading out of the reason for this enquiry?'

'If you must,' Feltsham said, in a quiet voice.

'You'll have to speak louder, sir, for I fear I am slightly deaf, from age and long speeches, don't you know, with most of them in foreign tongues.' This caused a ripple of laughter from the assembled group, but not from Lord Feltsham.

'I see nothing to laugh about, gentlemen, since I find myself having to answer spurious accusations regarding the bank's dealings.'

Loftus leaned forward, a cupped hand to his ear. 'What's, that you say? Please speak up.'

Feltsham repeated himself loudly in a rather annoyed tone.

'No need to shout, my dear chap,' replied Loftus, stiffly.

Looking down at the papers in front of him, the governor continued, 'We have a report from our accounts department. It states that while all the depositors did receive their funds and that taxes were paid, some interest payments that were due were not. It seems you ran out of capital and that adequate bank capital was never in place.'

Feltsham started to say something but Loftus put up his hand. 'Let me finish, sir. Then you may speak.'

After a short pause, Loftus continued, 'The accountants found that the main burden of financial loss was in fact to yourself, a considerable amount too by the time everyone was paid, which included your syndicate members. They are facing an enquiry themselves in Melbourne.'

Feltsham stood up. 'I demand legal representation.'

'No need, Lord Feltsham, apart from over some shortfall in interest payments, which we are sure you will make good on your return to England. This is to be paid by bank transfer to our accounts department here in Sydney who in turn will pass on the correct due amounts to the respective depositors. I should add that, if this fails to be done then you may face a custodial sentence. Do I make myself clear?'

There was a long pause before Feltsham answered, 'Crystal clear, but I still have a number of things I wish to do here in Sydney. These may take a month before they are completed to my satisfaction.'

'This board of enquiry feels that for the sake of social good order, the bank run did cause anxiety among your depositors, sir. They are still smarting from the experience. Indeed, we have a signed petition by them demanding a very strong action be taken against you and your syndicate members. No, Lord Feltsham, you leave New South Wales within the next week. Your fellow passenger will be a copy of this report to the London Authorities. I understand that we have enough black sheep, creditors, embezzlers and convicts in Sydney already, but if you wish to join them, in particular the latter, then we can accommodate you. I should consider yourself fortunate, through rank and privilege, to get off so lightly.'

For heartbeats the only sound in the courtroom was the rustling of paperwork and outside noises from the street below.

Feltsham adjusted his frock coat and began to button it up in a slow unhurried manner.

'Is that it? If so then I assume I can leave?'

Governor Loftus raised his hand, more in a dismissive attitude than a cordial gesture.

Feltsham stood, replaced his kid gloves and without another word turned and left the courtroom with all the arrogance that his ancestors had displayed at Agincourt.

# CHAPTER 29

'What is it, Tinker? We have not seen you for a day or two.' They were at the breakfast table, tea cups and cutlery clattering in the early morning sunshine.

Taking his seat, Tinker poured himself some coffee. 'I've been busy tiding up loose ends, Beth, because I am leaving to go on walkabout today.'

'This is very sudden, Tinker. As you know, we're preparing for our sailing to London next week. How long did you intend to go for?'

Tinker, his smile still in place, his hand on Beth's, said, 'For eternity, my child.'

All the china fell still. Justin looked up. 'Did you say eternity, Tinker?'

'Yes, for its time for me to see Shenkin again with Regan, Doctor Tarn, your father as well, Justin., and all that went before.'

'But you...'

Beth stopped him. 'You journey home, Tinker to your Dreamtime and the Land of the Dead.' There was a slight sob in her voice.

'The wind tells me so; we will travel in the clouds and disturb the dust across the bush.'

'To the mountain first, Tinker?'

'Yes, it is the place where the spirits depart for the Land of the Dead on the eastern side of the mountain. From this point, the gap to the Land of the Dead is bridged by an invisible tree. As I pass along this tree, I must undergo several tests, especially fire. Once I am on the other side, I will travel to the sky, remaining with the creative beings, the beings from the Dreamtime. You remember me telling you about this when you were a child and your pet rabbit died so that you knew nothing and nobody dies?'

'I do Tinker, I do,' Beth said, tears rolling down her cheeks.

'Then why the sadness? For is it not a moment of great joy that I will soon be back with Shenkin?'

'But you'll be leaving me.'

'Indeed. Until we too will met again in Dreamtime. Till then you will be safe in the loving arms of Justin, your husband, the father of your children. Temptations of the flesh are trials set by the spirits to test us and are only as deep as a layer of thin skin. If you want to see me again, remember that always. Do I make myself clear to you both?'

Hands clasped together, Beth and Justin nodded.

'Good then another loose end is tied off. Now I must make preparation. Firstly, I must bath to wash off this life so I can begin my walkabout to Dreamtime.'

'Where will we find you, Tinker, and when?'

'In three days' time this used body will be laying on a wooden platform up in the tree by the old sheep-cleaning stream, away from the hyenas. You will find a large flat stone beneath the tree; a shallow pit is already dug. Place my knees up tight to my chest and place the big stone on top of me. Cut my name into the stone Tallara Warron-Wurrah; not for me for the spirits know me, but for you unbelieving white ghosts of Europe,' said Tinker, with a chuckle.

'Tinker I can't, I…'

'How many kangaroos have we skinned out in the bush to eat with our witchetty grubs?'

'Many.'

'We just took their coats of this life off, which is all it is. Think of it as burying an old coat, for I will have no more use for it. I will be free.'

The room was silent; rays of the sun beckoned the start of another day while the sounds from the kitchen rattled its china plates. Outside, men, sheep and horses that had already been up since dawn slowed for their morning break.

'The place will be incomplete without you, Tinker.'

'But I will always be here, in the earth, the wind, the fresh morning air. Better that the spirits call me now than in London, because it would be such a long way to walk to Coolangatta Mountain.'

At this they all laughed. 'I just cannot believe that we are talking about it like this,' said Beth

'Please do as I wish, for are you not the daughter I didn't have?'

At this Beth threw her arms around this man who she loved like a second father. 'Of course I will.'

Three days later they went to the tree by the old stream. There on a platform of wood in the top branches of the tree they found Tinker, or at least they found his old coat, that he no longer needed.

Beth turned to Justin. 'It's time to go home, my dear, to see the children and settle our score with Lord Algernon Feltsham.'

# CHAPTER 30

A week later Captain Samuel Harrison welcomed them aboard the *Elizabeth*, bound for London.

'My apologies for not attending the opening of the Shenkin Charity Foundation Home. I understand Governor Loftus attended?'

'Indeed, and Lady Loftus too.'

'I am pleased the tribute was made to your father, Beth. Regrettably, there were last-minute sailing details to deal with and a crew to be hired and logged in and so many other arrangements, I'm afraid.'

'We understand, Samuel. It was good you were able to attend Tinker's funeral. It was the more important at the time.'

'It's strange not to see him at your side, Beth.'

'Every day I think the same, do we not, Justin?'

'Indeed, I expect him to walk in at any moment. It's a strange feeling of loss and regret that he is no longer with us.'

There was a few moments of silence from them all. Finally, Justin spoke, 'But tell me, Samuel, when do we sail?'

'On the tide, Justin, about three hours' time. I understand Feltsham left yesterday, also via the Suez Canal on the Orient Line, it's an iron screw steamship, the *Cuzco*. When your father was transported on the convict ship the *Runnymede* in 1832, it took three to four months to get to Sydney. Now, under steam via the Suez Canal, it's just sixty to seventy days at ten to twelve knots. We will soon be in the twentieth century; and already many things are changing in most areas of our lives.'

That evening, as the ship sailed out of the grip of Sydney harbour, they talked about the coming voyage.

'This will be a first for us, Samuel, going through the Suez Canal. What is it like?' said Beth.

'Well I can tell you about our passage. The voyage route we will need to take to reach the canal, but what it's like to pass through? I have no idea for this is my first time too.'

'How exciting, a voyage of discovery for us all then,' Beth said, adding, 'So to the passage, how long will it take to get there?'

'And what is its length?' Justin asked.

'Let our steward serve the main course and I will explain.'

In front of them lay freshly baked bread that steamed warm curling vapour up to the wooden beams overhead, with a plate of cheese to accompany the crusty bread. Ale was then placed on the table, much to Justin's pleasure, and some chilled white wine for Beth. Then the main meal, tonight it was chicken stew. In the centre, a cluster of spices, salt and pepper stood ready. The captain gave a small prayer of thanks for the food and for a safe voyage. Cutlery poised, Beth urged Samuel to begin.

Glass of ale in hand, Samuel began, 'Well first we go down the Tasman Sea into the Indian Ocean, then up to the Gulf of Aden and into the Red Sea, then the Suez Canal, which will take us into the Mediterranean Sea. So by switching from going around the Cape to through the canal, we save some five thousand miles. If we had full steam propulsion, we'd also do record time.'

'Get one on order, Samuel. We must stay competitive with our shipping line. Justin tells me that the British economy is thrusting ahead with its trading all over the world.'

'Is that so, Justin?'

'It is. Our overseas trade, due to an extensive commercial infrastructure, is selling its manufactured goods all over the world and we need a robust shipping industry.'

'I want BKSS to be in the front of that fast-growing economy,' Beth said.

'Consider the order placed. I will keep you advised. But first, the Suez Canal:

'It's one hundred and twenty miles long and will soon become a key trade route between Europe and Asia. A Frenchman named Ferdinand de Lesseps formed the Suez Canal Company in 1858. The construction of the canal took ten years, and it officially opened on 17th November 1869. It is a human-made waterway that travels north-south across the Isthmus of Suez in Egypt and connects the Mediterranean to the Red Sea, making it the shortest maritime route to Asia from Europe.'

The captain paused and took a sip of his ale, while the steward served desserts of peaches in chartreuse jelly.

'Ah! One of my favourites, Samuel, how thoughtful of you to remember.'

'My pleasure, Beth, as always. It took some time to locate fresh peaches but I felt it worthwhile just to see the look on your face.'

If Justin noted the intimate comments, he said nothing except to ask the captain to continue about the canal.

'Indeed. Well, it's a single-lane waterway with passing points at two locations, the Great Bitter Lake and Ballah Bypass. There is also a high toll charge to use the canal. This, I assure you, has been built into our cargo cost charges, Beth.'

'I am pleased to hear it. I would expect no less from my accountants on both sides of the world,' Beth said, with a smile.

'Of course. But let me continue, the history of a proposed canal goes back a long way. To the time of the Pharaohs in fact, and when Napoleon discovered evidence of an ancient canal, he ordered a topographical survey be done with the view of a possible canal through to the Mediterranean. But the Red Sea was thirty feet higher and they warned Napoleon of the possible flooding of the Nile Delta, and by then Napoleon had other things on his mind.'

'Fascinating, Samuel. What do you think, Justin?'

'I look forward to journeying back in time, if that's not a contradiction in terms.'

The meal over, they took a stroll along the gangway of the upper deck and bid farewell, for the time being, to Australia.

# CHAPTER 31

From Sydney to Suez was nine thousand five hundred nautical miles. At ten knots it would take them around forty-five days. While there were some spectacular sights on the voyage out, apart from a coal bunker stop, it was mostly monotonous views of open seas horizon to horizon. The evening meals of fresh meats, chicken, lamb and duck, washed down with cool ale and wine, made for a convivial relief from the monotony of the passage.

Beth and Justin spent their days in planning the legal action against Lord Algernon Feltsham. They needed to find the right solicitor and barrister to bring the court action statement and put the rest of the paperwork in order. Samuel studied his charts and learned about his steam engines from their chief engineer and his junior officers. At meal times, Samuel expressed the view that he wished he was back in the arms of the wind and sails and not on a smelly auxiliary ship, but that they were making good time.

Finally, they were at Suez and the mouth of the canal. Samuel Harrison carefully navigated the *Elizabeth's* sail along the canal, avoiding dredging ships and the sides of the canal, and in and out of the passing points.

At last they were in the Mediterranean and a course for London was plotted. That night they celebrated with some champagne and good cheers for the captain and crew.

After an uneventful sail up to the Pool of London, the *Elizabeth* was finally moored at the Royal Albert Dock at Gallions Reach. News of their arrival had been sent to their Portman Square home and also to Lady Hastings, via Lord James Hastings' flat in the city and his club.

To their delight, there on the dockside awaiting them was a carriage carrying Lord Hastings' crest. Saying their farewell to the captain and crew for the safe voyage, Beth fell gratefully into Florrie's arms. They were home.

The children were happy to have them home, and their nanny Molly was in tears at their return. All were sad at the death of Tinker and wanted to know the details and the children wanted to know where their grandmother and Aunty Jenny were.

Holding them tight, Beth said, 'Sadly Aunty Jenny is not well enough to travel at the moment but they have passage booked on a big steamship in two months' time, a nurse will travel with them so you'll see them then.'

'I'll bake a cake.'

'I'll get for them tickets for my next school cricket match.'

'Splendid.'

When on their own, Beth said, 'It's just as well they won't be here given the publicity the court case will cause, my dear. What progress do we have from the solicitor, Justin?'

'Well, you have met our solicitor John Hamilton-Smith a few times; he's one of the best in London and, as you know, my family's legal law firm right back to my grandfather's time. He tells me he's speaking to a number of leading barristers and will soon be in touch with us for a meeting.'

'Good I am anxious to get on with it. It's going to be a difficult time but I feel we have a strong case what with the statements and the enquiry reports from Sydney.'

'He'll contest it of course,' Justin said.

Beth nodded just as Florrie came into the room.

'You both look very serious, my dears, and we have the celebration of opening the Foundation in only a few days' time.'

'We do indeed, Florrie, thanks to your and Maria's efforts. I am most grateful for all your work on it.'

'Subject to your acceptance, a supervisor and staff are ready. James says he can persuade someone of importance to cut the ribbon on the day and give a small but effective speech.'

'So good of James, but I have something else in mind, my dear Florrie. Can we discuss it tonight when James is here?'

'But of course, Beth. I'm most interested to hear what you have in mind.'

As usual James was late home from his city office. 'Sorry, late again, Florrie dear. But pleased to see you and Justin here,' he said, kissing Beth and shaking Justin warmly by the hand. 'I was speaking about you both today, regarding the opening of the Charity Foundation Home, with a prominent member of the government. William Gladstone is euphoric over the Liberals win in the recent fiercely fought election, and in one of their largest majorities, leaving the Conservatives a distant second. I feel one of his frontbenchers should open the Shenkin's Charity Home, don't you, Beth?' James said, with enthusiasm.

'That's what we want to discuss, James.'

'Ah! Right. Fire away.'

'Justin, pour James a drink. In fact, we'll all top up our glasses.'

'Right,' Justin said, moving to the drinks cabinet.

Once the glasses were charged, Beth began. 'I want Tilley Collins to open the Charity Foundation.'

'Who is Tilley Collins?' James and Florrie asked, almost together.

Beth took a sip of her gin. 'Tilley is a cockney East Ender and one of the first to attend the Women's Feminist Movement. She had a good reason to become a member too, and better than most. At twelve she was raped, her mother a prostitute and her father in prison for robbery. At eighteen she was married to an abusive husband who beat and assaulted her on a regular basis.

'She was pregnant every year to eighteen months until her husband died of typhus in the local workhouse leaving her destitute with five children. They lived in a back street hovel off Mile End Road. There she took in washing and scrubbed floors from early morning to late at night. She is thirty years of age and on a very good day looks sixty. I intend her to be one of our first residents in the Foundation Home. No politician, Liberal or not, will grab the headlines, they have not earned the right to mark the plight of the underprivileged. She will cut the ribbon to her new home, we will invite the leading newspapers, in particular the *Times*, to write an article about her and her photograph will be in every broadsheet in Britain.'

For heartbeats it was silent, just the clink of glasses being lifted or put down.

Lord James Hastings stood up and raised his glass. 'Absolutely right, and so in keeping with Daniel Shenkin's legacy. I look forward to the privilege and honour of being there.'

'Thank you, James, and I hope you all feel the same?'

'Yes!' came the response as a pyramid of glasses clinked together.

# CHAPTER 32

At the Women's Feminist Movement the following night, Beth asked Tilley if she could speak to her after the meeting.

'I got a bleeding stack of washing to do I have, will it take long?'

'Perhaps half an hour, Tilley, no more, I promise.'

'Kids have to be fed, see, and put to bed like, all bloody five of them. I'll be working most of the night I will. Still since it's you.'

'Thank you, Tilley.'

After the meeting, Florrie and Beth helped to put the cups and saucers away, Tilley joined. Stacking the chairs they left three out in the corner of the hall.

Although it was still August it was beginning to get chilly in the evenings. Tilley sat with a threadbare woollen shawl around her cotton dress, a small world-worn figure in faded clothes.

'What's this all about then? Need some cleaning or washing done do you, ducks?'

'No, Tilley. We want to ask you to do something only you can do.'

'Blimey! That's a new one me.'

Beth explained about the opening of the Shenkin Charity Foundation Centre and that she wanted Tilley to cut the ribbon on the opening day. For some time nothing was said. The hall caretaker came into the room.

'I need to lock up, Lady Standish. Will you be long?'

'Can you give us a little longer, John, please?'

'Right you are.'

Still the room remained silent; then Tilley lifted her head very slowly.

'Bloody hell, I can't do that in front of a bunch of toffs, all dressed up in their bleeding Sunday best, looking down at me in my old cotton dress. If truth be known, it's my only bleeding dress.'

'I understand, Tilley, but Lady Hastings says she'll buy you a new outfit to wear.'

'That's right, whatever you would like to wear,' Florrie said.

Again for heartbeats no one spoke. Tilley wrang her hands over and over again.

'This here place is off Regents Park you say, a big bloody building?'

'Yes. A bloody big building, Tilley, and your home if you hear me out.'

'You're pulling my leg you are, having a bleeding laugh ain't you?'

'No, this is as straight as a beggar can spit, bleeding right it is,' Beth said.

'Never heard a lady speak like that. Sorry about my swear words, milady.'

'Tilley, I can outswear and outdrink you.'

Dressed in the latest fashion, Lady Hastings leaned forward, expensive perfume filled the air. 'Don't ask her to prove it or we'll be here all bleeding night.' It eased the tension of the moment as they all laughed.

'You're a pair you are, fit to make a monkey laugh, and that's the honest truth. Now tell me again what I have to do and what will happen to me if I do it.'

'On the day, you will be given a pair of scissors to cut a red ribbon across the main door. On each side of you as you walk up to the door will be Lady Hastings and me. I'll thank you, Tilley, then the press will take photographs and I will be interviewed by the *Times* and will tell them all about you.'

Tilley was startled. 'Bleeding hell, not everything I hope. Few things I'd rather keep quiet about, like. How do you think I got this here bloody shawl?'

'I won't mention anything that you don't agree to. You can read what I intend to say beforehand. Would that be alright?'

'If I could bleeding read it would be.'

'I'll read it to you slowly word for word.'

'You've always been fair to me, Lady Standish, right from that first evening when I called out "me too". I've been bashed about and ab… whatever it is you said, by my old man. I called it out I did from the back of the hall here. You came over to me later to see if there was anything you could do. Remember that I do. So's I trust you I does. After the snip, what then?'

'Well! How would you feel about being its first resident?'

'They won't want me up there, spoiling their nice clean places. Anyway how'd I get to my work in Mile End? I got to earn a living I have.'

'You'll have a job in the Centre. You'll have a three-bedroom flat with a kitchen on the ground floor. The job will be having the responsibility for the washing and cleaning of the Centre. You'll have two helpers that you'll be in charge of and give orders to.'

'I've never been in charge of a piss-pot before, never mind helpers. And there's the place in Mile End Road; I knows it ain't a palace, my hovel, but we call's it home, we do.'

'Give it back to the landlord, Tilley. Come to the Centre and there'll be no more rent to pay.'

'This is a bleeding dream this is. I'm going to wake up in a moment. But if it ain't a dream, then I'll take it. Can't wait to see the look on the landlord's face when I hand him the keys. The bastard's been putting up the rent every year he has.'

'That's settled then. On the other side of the building will be the caretaker's flat, name of Tom Clark no children no wife. He'll see to the locking up at night, any post or callers and, of course, the security of the building. There will also be a resident supervisor, and a doctor will call twice a week, so you will not be on your own.'

'Blimey! It's like a hotel.'

'We have tried to think of everything, Tilley. The other two Charity Homes are the same. However, there may be some unpleasant times due to a court case I am bringing against someone who wants to shut me down.'

Beth told Tilley all about Lord Algernon Feltsham, his activities in Sydney and his intentions in London.

'And you and your father trying to help the poor like you are. I'll give him a flea in his ear I will. You watch if I don't.'

'Thank you, my dear. We'll fight him together and win, for there's too much to lose for everyone if we don't. My father was determined to improve the lot of the underprivileged and disadvantaged in this hard world. He came from nothing, made good in Australia and wanted to use his success and money for others less fortunate.'

'Sounds a rare man he does and I can tell you I haven't much time for bleeding men.'

'We hope your experience improves when you meet Lord Hastings and my husband, Sir Justin Standish.'

'Cor! I'll be knee deep in toffs I will.'

'Yes, indeed, Tilley, sorry about that,' Beth said, with a smile.

'Tom Clark will get a carriage around to your place and help to load your bits and pieces. Tomorrow, if that's convenient?'

'Yes. But I still can't believe it's happening. It's all so fast, and that's the bleeding truth.'

# CHAPTER 33

On the day of the opening they were all lined up outside on the pavement. The traffic had been diverted and a number of constables were in attendance to make sure all went well; given that the chief constable was present, they were most diligent. The good and the great of London society, as well as two government ministers, were awaiting the opening ceremony. They had a letter from Prime Minister William Gladstone wishing the Charity Foundation every success and saying that he was pleased it was his government that encouraged such philanthropic gestures. Justin smiled as he read the letter. 'Political self-promotion, Beth, what can I say?'

'I have someone more honest to open the Centre, Justin. Shenkin, I know, would have approved.'

'Probably, but this letter will help your fight against Feltsham, will it not?'

Tilley refused to accept Florrie's offer of new clothes. Her simple cotton dress had been washed and ironed. She told Beth that her red raw hands from washing her customer's clothes had paid for the dress; she had earned it and she was going to wear it. On her feet she wore polished clogs. Beth understood. Pride and honesty was what the day was all about.

Tilley, flanked by Lady Hastings and Beth, moved to the front. Beth, a pair of silver scissors in her hand, turned to Tilley and handed them to her, handles outwards.

Everyone went very still as the ceremony began.

In a shaky hand, Tilley grabbed at them. Holding them tightly, she walked up to the red ribbon fluttering in the morning wind. She leaned forward and cut the ribbon to loud applause from the assembled crowd.

Beth gave a small speech declaring the London Shenkin Charity Foundation Centre open.

Turning to Beth, Tilley said, 'I've only bleeding gone and done it, I have.'

'You have, Tilley, and with great dignity too, thank you.'

While the press reporters were interviewing Beth and taking photographs of Tilley, much to her embarrassment, in the crowd three men were circulating while giving out leaflets.

Sir Justin Standish asked for one.

'There you are, guv, just printed this morning.'

'Thank you.' Justin read it quickly and shook his head in dismay. The headline read:

*WHO IS THIS MAN SHENKIN? WHERE DID HIS WEALTH COME FROM?*

*As honest respectable residents of London who are concerned whose names are on their buildings, we decided to investigate. We found some very disturbing facts. In late 1831, Daniel Shenkin was convicted of treasonable acts against the state and was transported to Sydney, Australia. He was sentenced to twenty years hard labour in the penal colony there. Following yet another criminal offence, he was sent to the Port Arthur Penal Settlement in Tasmania, a strict security prison, to complete his sentence. He escaped from the penal settlement with another prisoner and they embarked on a dangerous journey through the dense forests of Tasmania during which time, due to his recklessness, the other prisoner died, as did a friend, a successful sheep station owner, who was helping him to escape. Shenkin assumed his friend's identity, forged papers and took over the friend's sheep station on his return to Sydney. During this time he also hounded one of our aristocratic families, the head of which at the time was Lord Percival Hugo Feltsham who had moved to Australia to open a large sheep station to help the wool industry for England. Shenkin continually harassed Lord Feltsham and damaged his business interests, driving him out of Australia. Shenkin then took over Lord Feltsham's businesses. Daniel Shenkin: ex-convict, political dissident, fraudster, impostor and a man charged with treason.*

*Do we want his name on the edifice of our fine buildings? We say no. Close it down.*

Beth tore the leaflet up into tiny pieces. 'The bloody, bloody man, he must be stopped.'

Having read the leaflet, the government ministers were leaving, as were a number of other dignitaries. Slowly the crowd melted away, leaving Beth, Florrie, Justin, and Tilley Collins alone on the pavement.

'Well, we have food, tea and wine inside. Shall we retire to the main room?' Beth said.

Sitting around the table, Beth gave a deep sigh. 'Well, time to take the fight to Feltsham I think. What is our solicitor saying, Justin, has he briefed a barrister yet?'

'John tells me he's speaking to one of our leading barristers this coming Monday. Sir Fredrick Marshall, no less.'

Florrie put down her cup. 'James knows him quite well. He'll have a word with him over the weekend, if you like?'

'That would be most helpful, Florrie. Thank you, my dear.'

On Tuesday morning, Hamilton-Smith contacted Justin. 'He'll see you both tomorrow at midday.'

Beth held Justin's arm. 'Right, dearest, so we begin, do we not?'

# CHAPTER 34

The door burst open in his Middle Temple chambers, and in strode Sir Fredrick Marshall, gown billowing behind him, wig askew, which he immediately took off and threw onto his desk, revealing a bald head above brilliant blue eyes. His voice boomed from behind a whiskered face. 'Time is my enemy, my dear Lady Standish,' he said, leaning over to shake both their hands.

'Time, there's never enough of it. Due back in court in two hours, so let us begin. To start with, my clerk is not happy about you jumping my list of possible briefs. His list is as long as a hangman's rope, but it's time; how does one find the time?' he said, shrugging his broad shoulders. He was a big man with great presence. Very charismatic, he would make a fine actor. He revelled in his public nickname 'The great defender of the law'. The press loved him and attended his every case to record his oratory and take his photograph.

Easing himself into his chair he cast the blue eyes over them both. After a moment he spoke, 'James Hastings told me about your run-in with this, what's the fellows name?' he said, ruffling through a stack of papers in front of him. 'Ah yes! Lord Feltsham. Hastings and I were in school together, which is how you have managed to get in to see me so quickly. James has given me good financial advice over the years so *quid pro quo* and thank the playing fields of Eton.

'An action to sue for slander I see. I must tell you I do not usually take slander cases. To enlighten, "flim flam" is mostly hearsay and difficult to pin down, also the fee is not large and it does nothing for one's reputation. No, it really won't do. Has he murdered someone as a result of his slanderous words against you both, slit a throat or two, preferably in front of Buckingham Palace? It's the optimist in me, a good murder case, something I can get my teeth into?' Sir Fredrick looked from one to the other. 'No? Pity, murder is so much easier. Right, this is what I suggest; I understand that you, Sir Justin, and this Algernon Feltsham are members of the same club, is that not so?'

'Yes we are, Boodle's in St James's Street.'

'Not my haunt, I prefer White's, my dear chap, more conservative by far. Boodle's reputation is rather outlandish, but its membership is well founded by influential men of reputation, so it will suit our needs.'

Justin gave a well-intentioned laugh. 'We have certainly had some colourful members in the past. Did you know that Beau Brummel's last bet was placed there before he fled to France?'

'No, but I'm not surprised,' Sir Fredrick said, with a smile.

'This is my advice at no charge; put it down to my regard for Lord Hastings. To begin with, my clerk has prepared a background resumé of Lord Feltsham. It reads:

*Charged with non-payment of debts*

*Charged with violent drunken behaviour*

*Suspected of embezzlement, but not charged*

*A womaniser*

*Broken wedding engagements (2)*

*Suspect business dealings in wool industry – breach of contracts.*

*Arrogant in the extreme.*

'It's the last one that's his vulnerable area,' Sir Fredrick said, almost gleefully, his eyes sparkling in expectation of the trap he was preparing.

'Spread some gossip around Boodle's that Feltsham does not have the courage of his own convictions. He makes accusations against you both, through third parties, who are no more than hired agents, in particular against Lady Standish and her father. Let him face you directly, if he dares. If not he should be "black balled" from the club. Make sure you have witnesses around you when you meet, preferably a committee member who is prepared to press Feltsham to restate his accusations in writing, which is to be put on the committee notice board for all to see and vindicates his assertions.'

Justin looked aghast. 'Will he fall for that?'

'His arrogance suggests he will and he'll feel it's in the confines of his own club, not out in public. It's worth trying. When you have news, contact me again. I'll advise my clerk to set up an appointment at the earliest possible date. That should help his ulcer along. Delighted to have met you both,' he said leaning forward to kiss Beth's hand. 'The court calls, I regret to say, not that they can start without me.'

Wig back on, gown all of a flutter, Sir Fredrick made a dramatic exit. With his arms outstretched he looked like a large black bird of prey.

Beth turned to Justin. 'Will it work and are you prepared to do it?'

'He's the one with the experience, Beth, and it may well work; Feltsham is certainly arrogant enough.'

Boodle's was busy, many were staying in London for the weekend.

'The man's a bloody reprobate and no mistake, he makes these accusations against mainly my wife and her father, which resulted in a duel between us some while ago, at which he disgraced himself by firing early, would you believe?' Sir Justin said.

Thomas Laing, chairman of the club committee, was aghast at the revelation.

'If that is right, then we need to confront him.'

'Thank you, Thomas. I appreciate it. It's been so very upsetting to my wife.'

'Understand, my dear fellow, not the right behaviour for a member of Boodle's, not at all. What do you intend to do?'

Justin told him.

A cloud of cigar smoke greeted Justin as he sat next to a fellow member of parliament. 'The bill will go through, I'm sure of that. Incidentally, this Lord Feltsham I'm having a problem with, can you witness anything he may say when he next comes into the club?'

'Of course, if I'm here, I'll vouch for it.'

# CHAPTER 35

Feltsham finally came into the club on Friday evening; Justin had been waiting patiently all day. Walking up to reception, Feltsham asked the porter if there were any letters or messages, then went into the smoking room. Cigar lit, he began to read the day's papers. Justin went to find the chairman of the club committee; regrettably his fellow parliamentarian was not in.

'I intend to call him out, Thomas. Would you please witness it?'

'Of course, my dear chap.'

Finding chairs near to Feltsham, Justin ordered two whiskies.

Glasses in hand, Justin settled back into his Chesterfield. The steward placed a small table between them with a jug of water on it.

'Will that be all, Sir Standish, cigars maybe?'

'No, John, thank you. I'll ring the bell if I need to.'

Turning to the chairman, Justin raised his glass. 'Cheers.'

Only the clink of the glassware disturbed the silence of the 18th-century cigar-tarred smoking room.

'We've had a great deal to put up with from this slanderous man, now I find he is still a member of this club. Surely you understand my concerns, Thomas, that he may continue to spread these accusations. Not that he does it directly himself, for he does not have the courage to confront me with it. He hires others to do his peddling of these lies. I feel most strongly that he be "black balled" from the club. Lord Feltsham is a man of questionable reputation, not only here in London but in Tasmania and Sydney.'

The chairman took a sip of his whisky. 'I still feel he has the right to defend himself, Sir Justin.'

Lord Algernon Feltsham threw his empty brandy glass across the room in Justin's direction. 'Every word I have said here in this club, and elsewhere about your wife and her father is true. Your father-in-law cheated my uncle out of his assets in Australia. He died a broken man due to Daniel Shenkin.'

Thomas Laing slowly put his glass down. 'This is not the behaviour of a member of Boodle's, sir. You will put your accusations in writing, stating that you are acting in good faith regarding the wrong done to your uncle and the damage done to your family's financial position as a result. Once signed, the statement will be placed on the committee notice board for all the members to read. I should add, failing to do this will reflect badly on your membership of this club, do I make myself clear?'

Feltsham rang his bell; the steward came forward. 'You rang, sir?'

'Bring me writing paper, pen and ink, and be sharp about it.'

'Very well, sir.'

'I'll show you who is telling the truth over this, Standish, once and for all. Let the members read it. It will serve as further proof of Shenkin's fraudulent behaviour against my family.'

'John, please bring us two more whiskies and a brandy for Lord Feltsham, to help his Dutch courage along while he writes.'

At this, Feltsham scratched furiously on the paper, his face bright red with temper.

*This statement is to confirm to the members of this club that everything I have said about the convict Daniel Shenkin is true. The man was the late father-in-law of the Member of Parliament for Surrey Sir Justin Standish and father of his wife Lady Standish (nee Shenkin). Both were conspirators in Shenkin's swindling of my uncle, Lord Percival Hugo Feltsham, out of his assets in Australia by fraudulent means. I stand by every accusation I have made against this impostor, a man convicted of treason and sentenced to twenty years hard labour by transportation to the penal colonies of Sydney and Tasmania and who cheated my uncle out of his money, possessions and my family's inheritance, I intend to see justice done.*

*Signed this day the thirteenth of May 1880.*

*LORD ALGERNON HUGO FELTSHAM*

Having signed with a flourish, Feltsham threw the statement down in front of the chairman of the club. 'There it is. I wish it to be placed on the member's notice board without delay.' Then, placing the glass of brandy in front of Sir Justin, he said, 'When my legal people are through with you and your wife you'll need it more, I assure you.' Then, turning, he left the club.

'May I write a copy of this statement, Thomas? And if you would be good enough, after a week I'd like to take the original as evidence.'

'I don't see why not, Sir Justin, but do return it for my files.'

'Of course, and thank you.'

Leaving the club, Justin headed for Sir Fredrick Marshall's chambers.

# CHAPTER 36

Sir Fredrick Marshall was not a patient man. When they arrived at his chambers, he was drumming his fingers on his rosewood desk in his study.

'*Tempus fugit*, my dear Standish's, *tempus fugit*. Please be seated and tell me, was my ploy successful? Did Feltsham write a statement at your club, Sir Justin, and sign it?'

'He did. I have a copy right here,' said Justin handing over the paper. 'Also the committee will give me the original after it's been on the notice board for a week.'

'Excellent for we can now proceed with a case for libel. Your solicitor is preparing all the necessary background paperwork for me. We will then proceed to bring the case to court.'

'Which court?' Beth said.

'Why the Old Bailey, of course. Now that we can bring a case for libel, which is regarded as a serious crime, we can take it to the highest court in the land. It's almost as good as a murder, the press and their readers will love it. A scandalous society legal battle. Prepare yourself, Lady Standish, for some invasion of your privacy, I'm afraid.'

'It will be worth it to stop this man once and for all. What are our chances of winning the case, Sir Fredrick?'

'We have a strong case but I never commit myself this early on. Let us see what the defending counsel comes up with and who will be the barrister and the judge in the case.

'A libel claimant must establish that the words complained of are defamatory to him or them. Generally speaking, to prove defamation, you must show that a false statement was made, about you, to third parties which caused you damage and that it was written with malicious intent. In this case, and with this statement, we've strengthened our position considerably, but what will the defendant's barrister say? Possibly, that his client was manipulated into writing this statement. We say we have witnesses who will swear that the defendant wrote it to establish his credibility in the eyes of his fellow club members. However, you do see the possible arguments that may well come up in court. There are two sides to a legal battle: the plaintiff, in this case yourselves, who initiates the case, and on the other side the defendant, Lord Feltsham. He must answer the complaint and defend himself to the satisfaction of the judge and jury. That is to say, the judge decides law and the jury decides fact. In the middle of this maze the barrister stands up and represents his client's arguments armed with legal documents prepared by a solicitor. Interpretation of these documents forms the basis of the arguments. Oratory and conviction may sway the jury in their understanding of the facts, but not necessarily the judge's.

'Hopefully, in a month's time, depending on the court calendar, we will know the date of the trial, which judge is appointed and who the defending barrister is. At that time we will meet again, now I must fly.' An apt description given the black gown that flew through the office door.

'I too must go, I'm holding a Women's Movement meeting within the hour,' Beth said, adding, 'It's going to be a public circus, Justin.'

'Indeed, but the wheels are set in motion, and you have the right to defend your father's legacy.'

'Thank you, Justin, for your support in this.'

'We will prevail, my dear, I'm sure. Now I too must leave for the House. We have a vote to cast on workhouses for the poor, which must go through. We'll speak tonight at dinner about the day's events.'

Notes in hand, Beth addressed the women in the hall. 'Welcome to you all and thank you for coming. Firstly, given the publicity in the newspapers, I'm sure you are aware of my case for libel against Lord Feltsham. Those who know his lordship may understand, those who don't can consider themselves fortunate not to know him.' This raised some laughter.

'I have today sent a letter to the Law Society enquiring why women are not allowed to be on a jury.' Clapping rolled around the hall at this.

'The fact is, first, they must own land of a certain value and have the right to vote in parliamentary elections. None of which we have,' she added, 'Yet.'

Loud applause from everyone.

'I intent to use the trial as a rallying cause for women. Feltsham has been heard to say, "What difference does it make? She's only a woman." Well, he's about to learn the hard way that we women can stand up for ourselves. If any of you wish to carry banners outside of the Old Bailey, then you can be sure of maximum publicity for our cause.'

'Yes,' came the chant.

'Next on the agenda is the return to England of our main sponsor, Maria Alvarez, who tells me she has started a women's movement campaign in Argentina. Please welcome Maria.'

After much applause for Maria, and a short thank you from her for their welcome, she also explained that she was in London to support Lady Standish in her case against Lord Feltsham. This was greeted with thunderous applause. Given their full agenda, the meeting continued until quite late.

'Where are you staying, my dear?' asked Beth, as they prepared to leave.

'At Brown's. It's my favourite hotel in London; the history surrounding it is extraordinary. The Browns, for instance, were the valet and maid to Lord and Lady Byron; they got married and opened the hotel in 1837. It's made up of eleven Georgian townhouses, all very comfortable.'

'It's an excellent hotel I agree, but please come and stay with us at Portman Square. I know Justin would like to meet you, and it would mean we can compare notes at the end of each day in court.'

'That's most kind of you. I'd like that, but first I need to spend a few days visiting my sister Paloma.'

'Good, that's agreed then. I'll send a carriage for you in three days. Will that suit you?'

'It will, and thank you again, Beth.'

The days were busy for Beth preparing for the trial, meetings with the solicitor, reassuring the children and a thousand other public and domestic things to see to. Then Sir Fredrick advised them that the trial day was set.

'The judge is The Right Honourable Sir William Dickinson Webster, a strict by-the-book judge. We have met before in a few cases. He becomes cross if I spend a lengthy time on my delivery of certain points, but don't feel alarmed by that. I can use it to our advantage from time to time. There you are, you see, time, the devil in time. But remember you can win battles by knowing the enemy's timing, and then using a timing that the enemy does not expect.'

'Well put, Sir Fredrick, and the defence barrister?'

'A very good man, a worthy adversary, Charles Pitman QC is destined for a knighthood, they say, in the next honours list, formidable and persuasive. They will be interesting days in court, Lady Standish, so we must be ready for it, is that not so?'

'Indeed,' said Beth. There was a gleam in her eye at the promise of at last meeting Feltsham in a court of law, with no hired agents, or anywhere to hide.

# CHAPTER 37

The clerk of the court read out the charge, then asked Lord Feltsham if he was ready for trial.

'I am.'

'How do you plead to the charge?'

'Not guilty.'

The jury of twelve randomly selected laymen, often described as the 'corner-stone of the British criminal justice system' settled into their seats. Finally, the shuffling and seat scraping was over. Once there was complete silence, Judge William Dickinson Webster instructed the jury in the law and what was required of them, what they should take note of and to take note of anything he may say regarding the rights and wrongs of the law in this specific case before them. He then welcomed the two barristers by name to his courtroom.

'Gentlemen, we are in court nineteen of the Old Bailey, the highest in the land. I expect the same level from you both; you will adhere to my decisions at all times. Sir Fredrick, as the legal representative of the plaintive please state your case. However, I am well aware of your eloquence of speech, please keep focused on the main points of this case. Mr Pitman, you too will keep within the framework of the law, do I make myself clear? Sir Fredrick?'

'Indeed, my lord.'

'Mr Pitman?'

'Crystal clear, my lord.'

'Why do I not feel completely reassured? But I will be watching you both very carefully, like a cat watching a mouse. Sir Fredrick, please commence.'

And so it began. The public gallery was full, crowds had gathered outside and the press were everywhere.

Sir Fredrick's voice boomed out in his opening remarks, firstly he acknowledged his learned friend Mr Pitman. He then proceeded to lay out his case in broad strokes, addressing the jury as he did so. He talked for twenty minutes on his intention to see justice done, by putting before the court the libellous and slanderous remarks made by Lord Feltsham.

The judge looked up from his reading. 'This is not a closing summary, Sir Fredrick. Please keep to your client's reason for bringing the case to court: the facts, Sir Fredrick, just the facts.'

'I'm obliged to you, my lord. Passions run high when such injustices are evident.'

'You are doing it again, sir. Please limit your remarks to the actual facts of the case. The jury will disregard the last statement made by counsel, nothing is evident yet.'

Sir Fredrick raised his hands in the air. 'Thank you for pointing that out, my lord.'

'Nor is sarcasm, sir. Mr Pitman, your opening defence, if you please.'

'Thank you, my lord. Members of the jury, we will show that everything that Lord Feltsham has said was and is true, regarding the convict Daniel Shenkin.'

Sir Fredrick was on his feet. 'I protest, my lord, Daniel Shenkin had been given a Queen's Pardon and was no longer a convict.'

'Sustained.'

The arguments went on well into the afternoon. Beth was frustrated at not being able to speak out against the falsehoods that the defence was making, the twisted facts, the damning of all that Shenkin had achieved and had done for others during his time in Australia. But time and time again she was restrained by Maria Alvarez or others around her.

By five o'clock, the judge called an adjournment until ten o'clock the next day. Beth strode out of the court stopping only to thank Sir Fredrick for his efforts and ask if they could speak before the trial continued next day.

'But of course, Lady Standish. The first day is always most difficult, when you come face to face with the ridged British Legal system.'

At the door a press reporter asked if she had anything to say.

'Yes, go and find something else to write about, like man bites dog, or woman bites press reporter.' Maria held her hand as they faced the crowd outside. Abuse was shouted by a number of men and Beth's carriage was daubed with paint in large capitals: *GO BACK DOWN UNDER WOMANMONGER*. Her driver had been attacked and was holding a bloody handkerchief to his face.

'Peter, are you alright? Can I get you to a doctor?'

'No, your ladyship. I'll be alright. I'll get you home first.'

The drive down Newgate Street was slow due to the amount of horse-drawn carts, people and other carriages.

The driver made his way through the maze of streets back to Portman Square. There they were met by press reporters and photographers. The butler came out to force a way through for Beth and Maria, closely followed by Molly, the children's nanny, who was in tears.

'Molly, what is it? I'm sorry about all of this, is Sir Justin home yet?'

'No but the children are, Beth.'

'What! They should be at school.'

'There was an incident, something about the older children calling them names and hitting them. It was felt they should be sent home for their safety.'

'I'll come up to see them, Molly.' Turning to Maria, Beth said, 'This is the newspapers stirring up public interest two weeks before the trial even began just to sell their damn papers.'

'Well it is of public interest, a high society scandal, my dear, and the children hear their parents talking about it.'

'I suppose so and we have a long way to go, with a great deal to come out during the trial, which will make for much gossip, particularly among society who have nothing better to do.'

At that moment, Justin rushed through the door to the drawing room. 'Are the children alright? I had a message at the House saying they had been sent home.'

Beth explained. Together they went up to the children's rooms.

At dinner that evening, Beth was incensed at the day's events. 'It's the children I'm more concerned about, Justin.'

Maria nodded in agreement. 'I suggest you invite the parents for a dinner party to explain why you brought the case to court.'

'Can we, Justin?'

'I think it's an excellent idea before the trial is any further along. Thank you, Maria.'

'I'll send out the invitations tomorrow,' Beth said.

'Now go over the day in court, what did Sir Fredrick have to say?'

'Maria was my protector,' Beth said, holding Maria's hand. 'The crowd outside the Old Bailey was so large. Doesn't anyone work these days, Justin?'

'It's a case of public interest I'm afraid, my dear. You'll have to brace yourself. We knew this would happen and I regret it may well become worse.'

'I intend to keep the children at home until it's all over, Justin. Do you agree?'

'As you wish, my dear. It will certainly please Molly.'

The invitation went out and, one by one, people thanked Beth for the invite but were regrettably otherwise engaged on that day.

'The mealy-mouthed lot, they were pleased to come last Christmas, were they not?' Beth said. 'Well, to hell with them, and their insufferable attitude.'

The feeling in the household was that 1881 was not going to be pleasant and so it proved, with Beth trying her best to lift everyone's spirits. The fact was that they were isolated from society due to the scandal of the court case. However, Beth had no intention of changing course; she would defend her father's legacy until her last penny was spent and her last breath taken.

# CHAPTER 38

One newspaper the following day had the headline:-

*WE DO NOT NEED AN AUSTRALIAN CONVICT FAMILY
TO ACCUSE ONE OF OUR ARISTOCRATS, WHOSE FAMILY
FOUGHT AT AGINCOURT, OF LIBEL.*

The following editorial was just as damming in its portrayal of Beth and her rough sheep station upbringing in the outback of Sydney.

Beth ordered the paper to be disposed of, and that particular newspaper to be banned from the house. The *Times*, Justin said, was far more balanced in its comments but still questioned the rightfulness of the case.

Later at the Old Bailey Sir Fredrick was on his feet. 'The burden of proof lies with the defendant, gentlemen of the jury, not the plaintive. We are quite certain of the lies told by Lord Feltsham, told to gain money with false accusations against Daniel Shenkin and his daughter.'

'Do not lead the jury, Sir Fredrick,' the judge said in a rather annoyed tone.

'I must be allowed to state my case, your lordship.'

'Do not bandy words with me sir.'

'As my lord wishes, I'll rephrase the point.'

Pitman gave a slow smile. Beth and Maria looked concerned with the obvious dislike between the judge and Sir Fredrick Marshall.

Sir Fredrick rephrased the point.

'The rephrasing seems very similar to me, may I remind counsel for the plaintive that this is not a theatrical stage, but a court of law.'

'I'm obliged to you, my lord, for the reminder.'

So the day went on, soon witnesses were being called and cross-examinations began. Maria turned to Beth. 'I must leave for the sanatorium, my dear, but I'll return as soon as I can.'

'Of course, Maria, I'll see you then, use my carriage.'

'Here we are, ma'am, Bethlem Royal Hospital.' The heavy rain dripped off the end of the coachman's hat.

'I should not be too long, Robert. Take shelter in the carriage.'

'I'll find a place out of the rain, don't you worry.'

Maria hurried through the rain into the main entrance. The hospital was first known as Bethlehem Hospital, founded by an Italian, the Bishop Goffredo de Prefetti, as a monastery in 1247. He used it as a collection location to fund the Crusades and for the order of the star of Bethlehem, hence the name. It soon became known as Bethlem Hospital, and is Europe's first and oldest mental health hospital. But in the past its patients were subjected to some very harsh treatment, starvation, bloodletting and severe medical practices. The name finally evolved, by most people, into Bedlam Hospital. The word became associated with chaos and confusion, the saying 'It is all Bedlam' is well understood.

Maria hated the walk down the long corridors of the asylum, her shoes tapping out a feeble sound against the shouting, screaming background of the patients and the clunk of the iron-griddled doors opening and closing to the twist of the keys.

The warden unlocked the door to Paloma's room. Maria went to hold her but as usual she moved away quickly and sat on the edge of her bed staring at the wall opposite.

'No change then,' Maria said to the nurse-cum-warden.

'No she eats little and speaks less. More small noises than anything else, whimpering would be the best way to describe them.'

'I need to see the superintendent.'

'Very well, this way.'

'I'm sorry, Miss Alvarez, as I have said many times before we cannot release your sister without the permission of Lord Feltsham who committed her and pays for her care here.'

'Her husband by law.'

'We have him filed as her guardian under a confidential contract arrangement, made when Lord Feltsham made a substantial donation for repairs to the north wing. That was before I became superintendent here, as I have told you before I would have opposed the arrangement.'

'Are you aware of the case for libel against Lord Feltsham at the Old Bailey?'

'I am and I await the outcome with great interest given the bearing it will have upon your sister's residence here.'

'Then we understand each other?'

'We do.'

'Good,' Maria said, adding, 'Thank you again for your time.'

Standing, the superintendent offered out his hand. 'I wait to hear from you, Miss Alvarez, with, I hope, the best possible news for your sister's future.'

It was still raining when Maria came out into the fresh air. She gave a sigh then called the waiting carriage for the return trip to the Old Bailey.

Robert placed a cup of hot coffee in her hands.

'Thank you, how on earth did you manage to get it, Robert?'

'Spoke to one of the kitchen staff, ma'am, and I'm guilty of some flattery I'm afraid.'

'Well done, Robert. Not as good as our Argentinian coffee, but most welcome on such a day, thank you.'

The journey back was contemplative for Maria as she sipped her coffee, but strangely she felt more positive after her talk with the superintendent. She felt he was uncomfortable with the arrangements that had left her sister in such an unacceptable situation.

# CHAPTER 39

Maria took her seat bedside Beth. 'How is it going?'

'Heated. Pitman is a very able barrister, I regret to say his defence of Feltsham is firmly locked on to the fact that his client is telling the truth about Shenkin's background, therefore, no libel was caused. He is concentrating on the reason Shenkin was transported, his crime against the state and sovereign, that, in fact, if there is any libel it is one of the charges that could have been brought against Shenkin: one of Seditious Libel against the Crown.'

'My lord, I must object. We are not here to question the transportation of Shenkin but the libellous lies told by Lord Feltsham about Daniel Shenkin and his daughter.'

'Objection sustained. Keep to the reason for the case against the defendant, Mr Pitman.'

'My Lord.'

'Sir Fredrick has blocked any further pursuit of that line at least,' Beth said.

The case was adjourned at four o'clock and Beth braced herself for the difficult exit from the court. Press reporters surged forward once she was out in the main lobby of the courthouse. Beth said time and again, 'No comment', but it didn't stop the flash of lights from newly invented press photography for newspaper images, they lit up the coming evening, and blinded the eyes. 'Dear God what will they think of next?' Beth said shielding her eyes. 'Home, Robert, and watch the crowd's toes I don't want any one hurt. They would make harmful headlines, if someone was injured due to this "Womanmonger".'

The driver found it difficult to navigate the legs and feet, but soon they were on Newgate Street and on the way to Portman Square, where they found another crowd waiting for them.

'Maria, I feel you should not be subjected to this, my dear. I would completely understand if you wanted to go back to the peace of Brown's Hotel.'

Finally, the servants made a corridor for them and they were inside.

'How are the children, Molly?'

'Now don't you worry your head about them; they're fine, so they are.'

'Thank you, Molly. We'll be in the drawing room.'

'Right you are.'

'I don't know about you, Maria, but I'm having a gin and tonic, a large one. I had our wine merchant send over a case of wine from the Mendoza Province, also some Orange Liqueur Hesperidina from Buenos Aires.'

'The wine will be wonderful, Beth, thank you.'

The cold rain still fell, but sitting in front of an open fire began to restore their flagging spirits.

'Now, if I may, I'll stay with you here, Beth. We'll see it through together, and I understand from Justin that Lady Hastings is coming tomorrow. So a united front against the Feltshams of this world.'

'Thank you, Maria. I'll drink to that.' That's when a stone came crashing through the window.

The maid ran into the room. 'Are you alright, my Lady, Miss Alvarez?'

'Yes we're fine, Mary.' Beth had broken glass at her feet; a vase was shattered. The stone lay in the centre of the room, a paper wrapped around it. Two manservants rushed outside and searched the area.

Beth unwrapped the paper. *GO BACK HOME WOMANMONGER.*

'They're prepared to attack my own home with the children here too, Maria. It's just appalling. But it will not deter me, far from it. It only serves to make me more resolved to see it through.'

A little later Justin came into the room, wanting to know why the servants were searching the grounds around the house.

Beth explained and showed him the note from around the stone.

'This is completely unacceptable; I'll speak to the police commissioner tomorrow requesting around-the-clock protection,' Justin said, pouring himself a whisky.

'I think we must have safe sanctuary in our own home, for everyone's sake. The staff were very shocked, Justin.'

'I'll see that it's done, my dear. I assure you it will not happen again. Are you both alright?'

They nodded. 'It will take more than a stone to scare Beth, Justin, as you well know.'

# CHAPTER 40

'Why are there men with overcoats, rope and batons walking around the house, Mummy?'

'They're policemen, darling, to keep us safe from naughty men throwing stones at windows. It's a silly thing don't you think?'

'Yes I do, very silly.'

'Right I'm leaving for the House. Be careful going and returning from court, my dear, I'll see you this evening.'

'You too, be careful.'

'I will,' said Justin, holding the drawing room door open for Maria. 'Good morning, Maria. I'm just off.'

'Morning, Justin. I'll keep my eye on her. don't worry. We're going to the Foundation Centre before court, to see how Tilley Collins is getting along.'

'Now repeat my orders,' Tilley said, to her two young helpers. They called out their respective jobs for the morning.

'That banister in the main hall could still do with some more elbow work. I'll look at it again come midday, you see if I don't, and God help yourselves if it still looks dull.'

'You seem to have it all under control, Tilley,' Beth said.

Tilley turned sharply. 'You gave me a bleeding fright creeping up on me like that. Anyway, good morning, both.'

'How is it all going, Tilley? I intended to call around before now but what with the court case and everything… Is there anything you need?'

'Yes how about a bleeding whip for these two helpers of mine? Need to watch them all of the time I do.'

'Dismiss them then, if they're not doing the work.'

'No, I can't do that because it would mean I failed too wouldn't it? I'll get them to shape up I will, mark my words.'

'Alright, remember it's your decision, your staff.'

'I will.'

'And the caretaker, Tilley, all well there?'

'Yes, he's a nice bloke. Joins me for a morning cupper and a chat he does.'

'Good. We're just going to see the supervisor and then we're off to the Old Bailey.'

'Well most of my relatives were there in the past for one thing or another. Say Tilley sends her regards.'

'We'll see you next week, Tilley, when I'm sure the brass-work will look shiny.'

'It had bloody better be or they'll have sore arses.'

The journey to the court was uneventful until they arrived, then a crowd pushed around the carriage, rocking it quite violently. Finally, Robert managed to open the carriage door and forced his way through, with the help of the Old Bailey porters.

'It's like rounding up sheep in the bush,' said Beth.

'Or steering cattle into a corral,' said Maria. Hats askew, clothes ruffled, they were at last seated.

The council for the plaintive was on his feet addressing the judge. 'I would like to call Mr Thomas Laing as my first witness, my lord.'

'Very well.'

The court attendant called out, 'Call Mr Thomas Laing.'

Once inside, he was guided to the witness stand by the attendant. 'Please raise your right hand and swear on the bible.'

'I, Thomas Laing, swear by Almighty God that the evidence that I shall give shall be the truth, the whole truth, and nothing but the truth.'

Sir Fredrick Marshall looked up. 'Please state your full name and occupation at the moment.'

'Thomas John Laing, retired businessman, now the Chairman of Boodle's Private Members Club Committee in St James's Street London.' Given that before his retirement he was the head of one of London's most reputable investment houses he was completely relaxed and at his ease.

'I understand that you are a close friend of Sir Justin Standish, is that not so?' Sir Fredrick said.

'No it is not. Sir Justin is a club member and I listen to all their concerns, including Lord Feltsham's, for the sake of a well-run club.'

'Then you are completely impartial in this matter, is that correct?'

'Indeed I endeavour only to seek the truth, as it affects the club.'

'Excellent, very laudable. Did you witness the discussion between Sir Justin Standish and Lord Feltsham?'

'I did.'

'In your own words what did you think?'

'That Lord Feltsham was prepared to answer, in writing, what he had said verbally to other club members regarding Daniel Shenkin, his daughter and Sir Justin Standish.'

'This was made as a statement and duly posted on the club notice board. Is that correct?'

'It is.'

'My Lord, the original statement is before you and available to the court. It speaks for itself. No further questions of this witness. Thank you, Mr Laing.'

The judge looked up from reading the statement. 'Mr Pitman, your cross-examination, if you please.'

'Thank you, my lord. Mr Laing, when listening to the discussion between these two club members, isn't it true that Sir Justin Standish was in fact baiting Lord Feltsham into writing this statement?'

Sir Fredrick stood up quickly. 'I object, my lord, to the word baiting; my honourable friend is putting words into the witness's mouth.'

'Objection sustained. The jury will disregard that remark as hearsay and bias. Be careful, Mr Pitman.'

'I'm obliged to you, my lord.'

'We are in good hands, Maria. Sir Fredrick won't let him get away with anything,' Beth said.

For the next few hours the arguments ebbed and flowed until the judge called for an adjournment at four o'clock.

Press reporters crowded around Beth, firing questions at her.

'No comment.'

A court attendant came to Beth's side. 'Please, gentlemen, give her ladyship room.'

One of the reporters still pushed forward. 'This case is of public interest, Lady Standish, have you nothing to say?'

'Once again, and for the last time. No comment.'

Outside, someone threw rotten fruit at Beth, knocking off her hat and smearing her top coat.

Beth picked it up and threw it back at the man, hitting him in the face. The rotten fruit slid down his forehead and onto his cheeks then dripped off the end of his nose, ending in a blob on his white cravat. He stood there in a state of shock.

'Hats off, I do believe the man's about to cry,' Beth said.

The crowd laughed at the man's discomfort.

'Before you do it again, you should learn how to throw.'

Finally, they were in the carriage and away.

# CHAPTER 41

At Portman Square they found James and Florrie Hastings waiting for them in the drawing room. 'What on earth happened to your hat and coat, Beth?' Florrie said.

Having explained the incident there was laughter all around. 'A moment to treasure,' Maria said.

Glasses in hand and the fire aglow, they sat for a moment in peaceful reflection.

'We are prepared to be called as witnesses, Beth, to Lord Feltsham's poor social behaviour at the ball in our country house. Also to bear witness to his threatening posturing to a number of our guests. Which is why we have moved to our London house in Regent's Park. To support you in this matter, anything you need you have only to ask,' James said.

'That's very good of you both. I'll put it to Sir Fredrick tomorrow. He has, of course, agreed to call Maria to establish Feltsham's bigamy, but he intends to save it until his summing-up delivery.'

'What about disclosure to the defence, Beth?'

'He says he'll do so two days before. He'll tell the court that he'd only just heard about it and that it had a direct bearing on Feltsham's character.'

'Clever, if he gets away with it,' James Hastings said.

Beth nodded. 'He's a cunning devil, James. I think he'll get away with it alright.'

'And Feltsham's current wife, Beth, what of her?'

'Emily is still in Sydney, as I understand it, awaiting Feltsham's return.'

'If Feltsham is found guilty of bigamy, then his marriage to her will be declared void, poor woman.'

'Is that so, James, are you sure?'

'I am, it is unlawful under the Offences Against the Person Act of 1862 and it carries a maximum sentence of seven years.'

'Knowing Sir Fredrick, he'll go for the maximum,' Beth said.

'How long has the trial been going on?' asked Florrie.

'Six weeks now. The opinion is perhaps another two weeks will see it coming to a close, so a way to go yet, Florrie. My regret is that I am subjecting you all to this public glare of exposure. I am so sorry, my dears.'

'What are friends for if not to stand together at such a time?' said Maria. 'Remember I too have a score to settle with Lord Feltsham. It may well see the release of my sister.'

'I hope so, Maria.'

Lady Hastings leaned forward and held Beth's hand. 'We are steadfast in our friendship, Beth.'

'Thank you all. Mary, you can serve tea now.'

'Yes, ma'am.'

'This bloody House of Feltsham has been a source of trouble for so long. Firstly, the uncle to Shenkin and now this bloody Algernon Feltsham to Justin and I. He is nothing more than a complete waster, an out-and-out bastard. Sorry, Mary, for the language.'

'I hear much worse at home, ma'am, honest I do.'

'Thank you, Mary. It's good to know I'm in such company, my regards to your mother and father.'

'Oh! Cook wanted to know if Lord and Lady Hastings were staying for dinner, ma'am?'

'No we must return to Regent's Park. I have an early meeting in the city, but thank Cook, Mary.'

'Tell Sir Fredrick, Beth, that we are at his disposal.'

'I will and thank you both again.'

'Your carriage is ready, Lord Hastings.'

'Thank you, Robert.'

Once alone, Maria turned to Beth. 'It will soon be over. Nothing goes on forever. Even God can't stop time.'

'If only he'd stop Feltsham, but if he won't, I will.'

'Will you go back to Sydney once it's finished?'

'If the right verdict comes in, I'll put everything socially back in place here first. If I lose the case, I'll go straight back to Sydney and fight on there, if necessary. He hasn't got his slimy hands on BKSS yet. It won't be a stone; I'll throw a whole bloody sheep through his window.'

The door opened and Justin came in. 'Good evening, both,' he said, kissing Beth lightly on the cheek.

'How did the day in court go?'

'Arguments and counter arguments, my dear. The jury looked as bewildered as we were. Is that not so, Maria?'

'Indeed, in fact after one point of law by the judge I thought I was in the wrong courtroom.'

'And Feltsham, how is he standing up to it all?'

'As if he has already won the case, a smug look and with a smirk on his face.'

'It's all show, my dear.'

'Maybe, but his defence counsel Mr Pitman is good.'

'I have to go to my surgery in Surrey tomorrow, some problem with graffiti daubed on the office wall about the court case.'

'And our parlour maid Mary is getting abuse from her parents' neighbours about her working for a Womanmonger.'

'It's getting nasty. The press are inflaming public opinion to sell their papers while we are inundated with reporters wanting to interview us. I'm concerned about the effect on the children, Justin. This damn man is putting a blot on all our lives.'

Justin nodded as he poured himself a strong whisky. 'Does Sir Fredrick see an end in sight?'

'If he does he's not saying anything except possibly another two weeks.'

'I'm going to the Assembly Hall tonight, Justin, to make a formal appeal that women should have a vote. It's long overdue. Women's solidarity is gathering strength with more women of high social standing joining our ranks. I think over the next few years the movement will be so strong they will not be able to ignore us. Maria tells me that the Liberal Feminist Movement in Argentina is also gathering momentum, by way of female educators, medical doctors and social workers, many of which are first-generation women professionals in Buenos Aires.'

Justin smiled. 'Well I wish it success but, parliament is still mostly against it, my dear.'

'You'll change their minds, Justin. I'm sure of that.'

'Don't put such a burden on the poor man's back, Beth. He has enough to contend with dealing with this case. Is that not so, Justin?'

'It is, Maria, but I can cope with it.'

The maid came into the room. 'A message, ma'am, addressed to you.'

'Thank you, Mary.'

Beth read it through quickly. 'It's from the landlord of the hall I rent for our meetings, requesting a meeting tomorrow. Tell the messenger Lady Standish agrees to meet.'

'Very well, ma'am.'

'I have a feeling the landlord, a man named Wilson, is concerned about his precious reputation given the fact that he is dealing with a Womanmonger.'

# CHAPTER 42

'I regret, Lady Standish, but I must discontinue our business arrangement regarding the renting of the Assembly Hall for the purpose of promoting women's rights, and of course there's the current court case you have brought against Lord Feltsham.'

'I see.'

'I realise this is short notice but the hall will be closed from tonight.'

'I have a meeting arranged for tonight, Mr Wilson, and it will be held here, door locked or not.'

'But how?'

'Outside in the street. It will help to bring attention to the plight of women. I will, of course, cite you for closing your doors to us, although we have legally paid the rental in advance.'

'But that's preposterous, madam, a woman telling a businessman what he can and cannot do. You would not dare,' Wilson said, in a very angry tone.

'Watch me. Come along tonight; you can help explain to the police why there is a public disturbance in the street.'

Later that evening, Beth addressed the meeting on a wet pavement and explained why they were outside in the cold rain.

'It's the sort of thing my old man would do, bastards they are, all of them.'

The policeman, swinging a truncheon in his hand, pulled up the collar of his great coat against the wind. 'Now then what's going on here, you're causing a public ruckus you are, so move along before I call a police wagon to take you all to the local jail.'

Beth stepped forward. 'I hope it's a big jail because this is a large gathering. Does it have water, food and, of course, lavatory facilities?'

'Get back to your homes and kitchens, where you belong, and be quick about it.'

'But that's the whole point, officer. We don't want to spend all our lives in a kitchen, would you?'

'You're Lady Standish. I recognise you from the newspapers.'

'I have that honour.'

'Then you should know better than to encourage these women in civil disobedience.'

'I was the one who called the meeting, officer. We would rather be inside but the doors have been locked to us.'

'Jock Wilson is the owner. He lives locally; I'll have him brought here,' said the policeman.

An hour later, Wilson, keys in hand, fumbled with the lock. 'I have a right to cancel my arrangement with this woman. It's not as if she is a man.'

'Sort it out legally tomorrow; tonight I want them off the street.'

'Thank you, officer.'

'Don't thank me, just get in the hall and off the pavements, and get off the road to let the carriages pass.'

Later at Portman Square, Beth sat down in the drawing room and felt like bursting into tears, but she was determined not to feel like a helpless woman.

She sat very still, her hand gripping the side of the chair. 'Dear God, have I taken on too much?' The court case, the Women's Movement the general upset to everyone she loved. 'Take a deep breath, Beth.' What would Shenkin have told her?

'You started it, you believe in it so bloody well stay with it, girl.' That's what he'd say. *So it shall be.*

Justin came through the door. 'How has your day gone, my dear?'

'Difficult.' Beth paused. 'You're very late back from Surrey, problems?'

'The office walls were daubed with obscene graffiti about us and the trial.'

'I've just been going over it in my mind. I know how terrible it is, Justin, but I really must go on with it.'

'Of course, we've gone too far now. Let's hope Sir Fredrick can soon bring a successful end to it.'

# CHAPTER 43

'I'll call Lord and Lady Hastings; it will bear witness to Feltsham's social behaviour.'

'It will all help, will it not?'

'Indeed.'

'Good of them to offer. Incidentally, I think we are coming to a close in the case and I am preparing my summary, at which time I will ask Maria to bear witness to Feltsham's treatment of her sister and their marriage. Would his current wife or her mother be prepared to be a witness?'

'The wife, Emily, is a nervous timid soul. It would be too much for her and the mother is very protective.'

'Well it would delay the trail anyway given the journey time from Sydney to London. No, I think Maria's paperwork confirming the marriage will be sufficient.'

'You must be tired, Sir Fredrick, are you not?'

'It's what I do, dear lady, the main stress of the case is yours and Sir Justin's. The law is unbending. It grinds slow but fine; one keeps stirring the handle in our favour.'

'I think under that gruff exterior you have a warm heart, Sir Fredrick Marshall.'

'Dear God! Don't let anyone hear you say that or I won't be able to go into court again,' he said, leaning forward and kissing Beth's hand. 'Let it be our secret.'

'Always the showman, the polished actor.'

'It's what I excel at, Lady Standish. Now off you go, I must return to the preparation of our summary.'

Two days later the summation was indeed polished. The Hastings gave their evidence and Maria produced the marriage certificate of her sister to Feltsham.

The superintendent of Bedlam was obliged, under oath, to confirm his arrangements with Feltsham, which established his bigamy and his attempt to cover the marriage up. Many on the jury shook their heads at the charge of bigamy.

The defence was asked if they wished to cross-examine the witness.

Pitman stood up. 'No questions, my lord.'

Feltsham turned to his counsel. 'But...'

Pitman cut him short, 'Do want it to be repeated?'

Sir Fredrick continued with his catalogue of Feltsham's background of accredit accusations, gambling debts and a number of court cases regarding assaults on fellow gamblers.

'Any cross-examination Mr Pitman?'

'No questions at this time, my lord.'

By late afternoon the judge asked the jury to make their deliberations and to come to a verdict.

At exactly four o'clock, only thirty minutes later, the jury were back.

The court attendant handed a paper to the judge.

'Will the defendant please stand?'

'On the charge of libel. Guilty.'

'On the charge of slander. Guilty.'

'On the charge of bigamy. Guilty.'

'After further deliberation the sentencing will be carried out tomorrow at ten o'clock,' the judge said. 'Court adjourned.'

Beth turned to Sir Fredrick. 'We are most grateful to you.'

'We are indeed,' said Justin, adding, 'What sentence will the judge impose, do you think?.'

'It's the bigamy charge that is the capital offence; it carries a five to seven years prison sentence. Judge Webster is very strict on capital offences so I expect a custodial sentence together with a steep fine, and remember Feltsham will also have to pay all court costs. It will ruin him financially; there's no denying that. So I'll see you both here tomorrow and, of course, yourself, Miss Alvarez, I trust this outcome will soon have your sister released and back in the loving care of you and your parents.'

'Thanks to you, Sir Fredrick.'

'I'm just a hard-headed old barrister doing his job as best he can,' Sir Fredrick said, winking at Beth.

That evening at Portman Square they held a small celebration that included all the servants. Champagne was poured, glasses raised, and Beth thanked everyone for their loyal support.

The following day in court the judge addressed Lord Feltsham. 'Will the prisoner stand please?' After much chair scraping and dust lifting, Lord Algernon Feltsham was on his feet.

'Lord Algernon Hugo Feltsham, you have been found guilty on all charges. Do you have anything to say before sentencing is carried out?'

'No, my lord.'

'Very well. On the charge of bigamy you are sentenced to five years imprisonment and fined. On the lesser charges you are fined substantially on both counts and also ordered to pay the court costs. Separately, I am submitting a request that you be stripped of your titles by an act of parliament.' The judge paused for a moment to let this sink in, then continued, 'You will be taken from here to a holding prison for two days, and hence to Pentonville Prison where you will serve your sentence. Take him down.'

The hushed silence around the courtroom was palpable. For heartbeats no one spoke or moved. Beth held her breath, her eyes filled with brimming tears. It was all over. Maria leaned forward and gripped her hand, while Florrie had an arm around Beth's shoulders. 'Let's go home,' Florrie said, in a dry whisper.

'I must see Sir Fredrick Marshall first.'

'Of course, we'll wait in the hallway for you.'

Black gown flowing, wig at an angle and holding a fist full of papers, Sir Fredrick glided into the room.

'Thank you for saving Shenkin's legacy, Sir Fredrick. I can't begin to put it into the right words, I shall be forever grateful.'

'My wife told me not to come home if I lost this case, my dear. So what's a mere man to do?'

Their shared laughter rang out like Christmas bells as Sir Fredrick threw his wig in the air.

# CHAPTER 44

At Portman Square it was indeed like Christmas: flags, balloons, bunting and a large bowl of punch. Justin came home early with best wishes ringing in his ears from his fellow politicians on both sides of the House. The celebrations went on late into the night.

For Feltsham there was no such jubilation. 'Remove your clothes and be quick about it. We're giving you a shower and delousing procedure,' said the prison guard.

'How dare you address me in such a fashion, unhand me immediately.' This was Feltsham's first mistake. A baton came out of the guard's belt and sank deep into Feltsham's stomach. All the wind left his body and he dropped to the wet floor in a heap. He struggled to his feet. 'I'll report you to your superior; tell him I want to see him, do you hear me?' That was Feltsham's last mistake, everything went black in a whirlpool of pain.

A day later he came around on the floor of a dark damp cell, His stomach was a bag of bruised muscle and tissue, his right eyebrow was split open and his lower lip swollen out of shape. He could hardly see or swallow, and standing was too painful.

A shutter in the upper part of the door opened and a tin plate of food was thrown into the cell, scattering its contents around the cell floor. The rats got to it before he could.

The gaoler called out, 'Welcome to Pentonville Prison, your lordship.' The laughter drifted away as he walked out of the cell area of the wing Feltsham was in. He had been unconscious for a day and a half; he tried again to stand but failed.

Pentonville Prison is located in Islington, North London. Built in 1842 it pursued the ideas of reformers John Howard and Elizabeth Fry. The latest technology was in use, modern ventilation was introduced, also some heating systems. Even in the face of hard and cruel treatment of prisoners it was regarded as a model prison. All future prisons were based on the same build system, including the notorious Port Arthur Penal Settlement on Tasmania, where Daniel Shenkin was held all those years before. Ironic, since it was Feltsham's uncle, Lord Percival Feltsham, who had sent Shenkin to the Port Arthur Penal Colony, to a prison based on the Pentonville model, where now Algernon Feltsham would meet his fate.

In North London's Pentonville Prison, prisoners spent twenty-three hours a day alone in their cells the 'silent system' was in strict force. Reformers felt that this would teach prisoners the errors of their ways, since they would have ample time to reflect on their crimes and soon change their ways. Failure to be silent at all times resulted in punishment by whipping.

Feltsham was on a steep learning curve, regardless of his beatings he was put to work the following day. Now dressed in the prison's broad-arrow marked clothes, of hard-wearing cheap-quality fabric, he found the coarse material irritated his normally silk-wrapped skin and at first refused to wear the clothes, so the gaolers left him naked for one week. On the eighth day he wore the prison clothes eagerly.

A guard led him to a long shed. 'You're going to walk this treadmill for the next four hours to power the prison machinery. Do your legs a power of good, then we'll find some other hard labour work for you, got it?'

'But I...'

'Talking are we? That's a punishable offence, that is. Harry, make sure he does six hours on the mill.'

'Right, six hours it is.'

Straw bedding or not, he slept that night until breakfast was thrown into his cell. He did more treadmill work and picked oakum for twelve hours until his soft hands bled.

After a long hard month in the prison, his defence barrister, Pitman, came to see him.

'I have bad news and very bad news. You've been stripped of your titles and are now officially Mr Algernon Hugo Feltsham. All your assets including your country house are being confiscated to pay your debts. As you know, your younger brother George died some years ago in the army; however, I regret to tell you that your sister Greta has contracted tuberculosis. She is not expected to see out this year. It's a great deal to come to terms with. I'm sorry to be the bearer of such news. Financially, I have listed you bankrupt, effective this week.'

Feltsham remained still for a long moment. Only the sound of cell doors clanking open and closed disturbed the silence.

'Did you hear me, Algernon?'

'Unfortunately I did.'

Pitman stood. 'I'll come to see you again in a few weeks' time.'

Instinctually, Feltsham knew this would be the last time he would see his former defence counsel.

# CHAPTER 45

At Portman Square, Beth received a letter from Maria, it had taken over a month to reach her by the Travelling Post Office. Eagerly, Beth read it to Justin.

*My dear both,*

*I trust this letter finds you both well.*

*Sadly my father died last month but at least he saw his youngest daughter back home, thanks in great part to you, Beth. With no sons, everything has been left to me, the houses in Buenos Aires, Santa Rosa and Viedma together with all the Haciendas and ranches across the Pampas. It is a big responsibility, but if a man can do it, so too can a woman, is that not so, Beth?*

*I have also been appointed the first woman president of the Cattle Association in this part of Argentina – we progress.*

*Paloma makes slow but steady progress. My mother sits with her for long periods of time, so we have hopes for her recovery.*

*I hope we will see you both one day here in Argentina. Please send me your news; we now receive mail at the rail head in Buenos Aires for collection.*

*Much love,*

*Maria*

*\*PS I have increased my quarterly donation to the Women's Movement from £250 to £300 I know you will put it to good use. 'M'*

'How generous, what will you use it for?'
'I'll discuss it with the committee; I'd like to purchase a printing press to print the first woman's newspaper, to be called *Women's Equality.*'
'Excellent, it says it all.'

'Well that's my thinking, members, can we vote on it?'

Without hesitation they all put their hands up. 'Thank you I'll place an order immediately.' Six weeks later the hall workshop shuddered with the sounds of printing thuds, which was music to Beth's ears.

'The paper will be issued free of charge, any donations will be gratefully accepted, while the editorial will cover women's concerns and the need for a vote. The paper will also carry articles on cooking, dress patterns and children's wellbeing,' said Beth.

The second printing press arrived soon after, and distribution soon moved out of the East End into the greater London area. It was a success. It resounded with the populace who could read, who then passed on the contents of the paper to others.

'And you are?' said Beth

'A member of the National Society for Women's Suffrage formed ten years ago, and we wish to associate ourselves with your Women's Movement, my dear, are you prepared to discuss such an arrangement?'

'I'll speak with the committee members; can you give me a week?'

'But of course.'

Beth addressed the Women's Movement. 'We will soon be in 1882, ladies, and their recently appointed chair is a very forward-thinking woman and could give us a louder voice in parliament and even court circles. This is an opportunity to advance our views on votes for women. I urge you to take it.'

They did.

The vote was carried unanimously and the joining of the two was announced in the following month's newspaper.

At a number of social events, Beth was congratulated by many leading society women. 'So brave, my dear, so very brave, I would like to support you but my husband is completely opposed to the notion that women should have the vote.'

'I understand, Lady Chambers. You have a daughter I believe, is that so?'

'Indeed, Beatrice is the centre of my life, Lady Standish.'

'Not when she is married, then, I regret to say, she'll become her husband's chattel, as will your grandchildren,' said Beth, walking away, leaving Lady Chambers in a deep contemplative mood.

'Sorry to disturb you, John, but might I have a word?'

'Of course, my dear, we need to leave anyway. I have an early meeting in the House of Lords tomorrow.'

Once in their carriage Lord Chambers asked his wife what was on her mind, she told him.

1882 and 1883 saw Algernon, if not happier, at least becoming hardened to prison life. The gaolers were tiring of ridiculing him or punishing him for the smallest infringements of the prison rules.

'Start scrubbing the floors, Algie, until I tell you to stop.'

Feltsham bent to his task, at least he was not on the treadmill tearing the skin from his hands or splintering his fingernails, picking oakum.

Stepping on the carbolic soap, Algernon slid across the floor and down the iron steps to the lower ground floor. Standing, he promptly fell down again as the femur of his left leg came through the skin.

'Look on the bright side, Algie, it's a rest in the prison hospital for you. Frankly, they're not the best at setting bones, but you may be alright, see you in two or three months.'

The pain was excruciating, as they set the bone back in place. Forcing him to try to walk again in only two weeks, he broke the femur again. In three months, with the aid of a walking stick, he was back in his cell.

'Algie, good to see you back. No treadmill for you with that there leg but I've saved you lots of oakum rope to pick. I know you'll be pleased with that, so get on with it over at the shed. Careful you don't fall down the steps,' the guard shouted after him.

So his third year began. Twelve hours later, he was back in his cell, hands ripped and bleeding and most of his fingernails gone. He said nothing.

'We've taken delivery of a lorry load of new oakum rope, Algie, should keep you busy for years.'

The calluses on his hands got deeper, cracking the skin open on his fingers causing painful infections. He said nothing.

# CHAPTER 46

'When will the wedding be, Tilley?'

'Next month. I needs to find someone to give me away I does. My drunken old dad is bleeding useless.'

'Sir Justin will do it, Tilley, and Lord Hastings can be one of your ushers. I'll speak to them tonight.'

'Blimey! You can't do that, Beth.'

But Beth did, and they did.

Both Tilley and Tom Clark looked the picture of happiness on the day, while outside the small church a woman at Beth's side said, 'Isn't that the MP Sir Justin Standish giving the bride away?'

'I do believe it is,' said Beth.

'The bride must be of noble birth, wonder who she is?'

'Noble birth indeed, for her and others like her, are the backbone of the British Empire.'

From that day on, Tilley and Tom would run the London Shenkin Charity Foundation together.

In response to a knock at the door, the man sitting in the centre of a long table spoke, 'Come in.'

'Prisoner Number 8221 Feltsham, sir.'

'Please sit down.'

Feltsham did so.

'We see you are the former Lord Feltsham, therefore well-educated, and we would like to ask some questions.' After a pause he continued. 'Every month we of the appeal board, that is say myself and fellow appeal judges, consider prisoners who may be suitable for early release. Do you have anything to say in this regard?'

'No.'

'This is your fourth year of a five-year sentence at Pentonville. Do you wish to make any statement regarding the prison?'

'No.'

'Would you wish to comment on your treatment during these four years?'

'No.'

'Would you commit the same crimes again? If not then why not?'

'No, it is now irrelevant.'

'Are you remorseful of your crime?'

'I would have preferred not to have experienced the last four years.'

'That's not what we're asking. Can you elaborate further?'

'No.'

After some moments and discussion with the other judges, he was asked to wait outside.

Some thirty minutes later he was again sitting in front of the appeal judges.

'We have decided to uphold an appeal. You will be released one year early. Do you wish to say anything?'

'No.'

'You will be given your clothes and personal items back and released in one month's time, any comments?'

'No.'

The following month at the breakfast table in Portman Square, Justin folded his *Times* newspaper into a quarter and handed it to Beth. 'Bottom left, an interesting news item, my dear.'

Putting down her teacup Beth read.

*The former Lord Feltsham was today released one year early from his five-year prison sentence here at Pentonville Prison.*

*Apart from our press reporter, no one was there to meet him. He reported that Feltsham cut a very sad figure. Ill-fitting clothes hung on him like a scarecrow. He walked with a pronounced limp, one eye partly closed and what appeared to be a broken nose. A broken man too, in every way, physically, emotionally and spiritually.*

*Our reporter helped him reach the Islington workhouse, his only abode. He has paid his debt to society and no matter what his crimes, this paper wishes him some hope for the future.*

'Do you know anyone at this workhouse, Justin?'

'I can make some enquiries.'

'Thank you. I'd like to visit him; what do you think?'

'Your decision, my dear, and I know it's not to gloat.'

Within a few days a meeting was arranged with the supervisor of the Islington workhouse.

# CHAPTER 47

'This is quite irregular, Lady Standish. I must insist that if he objects to seeing you, then you must leave.'

'Understood and agreed.'

The workhouse was cold, damp and dark. It had an overwhelming smell of urine and vomit. Voices called out from the darkness as Beth walked past each dormitory. 'We call it the workhouse howl, Lady Standish,' said Andrew Symons who had been master of the workhouse for the past five years. 'Be careful where you walk, milady. The inmates tend to sleep in the corridors sometimes.'

'Thank you, I'll be careful.'

Symons was a man full of his own importance and empty of any pity. His mantra, one that he repeated over and over as Beth followed him down the stone cold corridors of the workhouse, was, 'They must learn to work; they must learn to work.'

Finally, they came to the back of the building which had a small garden, a rose garden, Beth noted.

'Someone to see you, Feltsham.'

Beth stood at the entrance to the garden. 'Lord Feltsham, may I talk to you?'

'It's a long time since someone called me that,' he said, turning with some effort as he dragged his leg around.

The surprised look on his face was matched by Beth's shock at the sight of Feltsham up close.

For heartbeats they just stood there until the silence was broken by Symons.

'Will you need me to stay?' he asked.

'No. I'll be fine.'

'The lady will be quite safe. Not only can she outrun me, but she can also outwalk me.'

When he had left, Feltsham faced her. 'You're the last person I expected to see here. You'll forgive me if I don't address you by your title; you see I lost mine some while ago, careless of me, having had it in the family for so many hundreds of years.'

'This is the last place I expected to be, and my title was by an act of marriage, very new by comparison.'

'You're here to gloat?' Feltsham said, in an empty flat tone.

'No. I'm here to talk, if you have the time?'

'It's the one thing I have plenty of, Beth Shenkin. It is Beth Shenkin is it not?' said Feltsham.

'It is.'

'Regarding time, I am blessed with time, the days hours and minutes of it.'

'Beth please.'

'Have I earned the right to call you Beth after our travels along the jolty road of our own making?'

'I think so, if you allow me to call you Algernon,' Beth said, adding, 'please.'

They talked well into the afternoon.

'May I come again?'

'Not here, I am taking up residence on one of the London Park benches. Regrettably, Symons tells me I must leave in two weeks.'

The master came through the door. 'I'm afraid you must leave, milady, we'll soon be closing the main doors.'

'I'll keep in touch somehow,' said Beth.

'Until our next meeting in Regent's Park then,' Feltsham said, with as much flourish as he could muster.

Walking back along the dark corridors, Beth looked into one of the dormitories. The room was cramped, the beds squashed together and there was very little room to move.

'The place is empty, Mr Symons. Why is that?'

'The inmates are woken early at around 5am, and apart from prayers and meals they are expected to work until 8pm before returning to their beds.'

Beth's face registered her alarm.

'This is a workhouse, Lady Standish. All must work to earn their keep, unless, like Feltsham, they are unable too due to ill health or disability. Which is why Feltsham will have to leave in a few weeks' time.'

'But what will become of him?'

'Like most paupers, tramps or vagrants they die on the streets of London or other cities. We uphold the Poor Law Act, milady, but there's only so much we can do.'

A child's cry pierced the air.

'You have children here?'

'Yes, the women and children are kept in a separate part of the workhouse. Babies are born here, but few survive the first year of birth, for the sanitary conditions are not conducive to the very young, and, of course, the mothers must work if they are to stay. I see you're shocked, Lady Standish, but the conditions are deliberately harsh, so that only those in desperate need ask to come here.'

'What of the food and milk for the babies?'

'Very restrictive, we are underfunded, milady. We do the best we can. Children under the age of two can stay with their mothers, but you must remember that by entering a workhouse, paupers forfeit their responsibility to their families; the state takes over.'

'But if they had little choice due to their living conditions or abusive husbands and no say in its correction because they have no vote, what then?'

'Not my responsibility, milady, I'm pleased to say.'

'Someone should take up their cause. I'll certainly raise it at the next meeting of the feminist movement.'

'As I said, your visit here was most irregular, so I ask you not to mention this workhouse by location or my name.'

'We cannot hide forever, Mr Symons. It needs changing and for the better.'

# CHAPTER 48

'There are some two thousand workhouses in the country, Justin, enabling over ninety thousand places to hold paupers in the most appalling of conditions. They are made to work from early morning to late evening, under the watchful eye of the people running the place that was, under the Poor Law Act, intended to provide work and shelter to the most poverty-stricken people in society, to deal with pauperism where needed. But what it has become is nothing more than a prison system, holding the most vulnerable in society. Forced child labour, long hours, malnutrition, beatings and neglect.'

'The government do the best it can, my dear, but it is a huge problem. With so many in poverty, we could fill twice the number of workhouses, if we but had them available.'

Beth raised her arms in dismay. 'The protests from many leading people go unanswered and the years pass. It's people's lives, Justin. Their very existence. The novels of Dickens hang in the air like the ghosts of Christmases past, but nothing is done. Given all this, what will become of people like Feltsham?'

'He'll have a hard difficult time, Beth, there is no doubt about that. The streets of London are cold and harsh.'

'I intend to protest outside every workhouse in London. My women will carry banners declaring our dissatisfaction with the system and demand change.'

'I'll sound out the thinking in parliament, but I'm not very hopeful of support, Beth. The Poor Law Act was a hard bill to pass in the first place.'

'Thank you, Justin.'

'You have another few days, Feltsham, and then you are out,' the guardian said.

'But where do I go?'

'Not my problem, or that of the Workhouse Union. You cannot work so are useless to us. We're local businessmen and must make a profit, the workhouses take up much of our time as it is, without losing us money as well. Three days at the very most then out, is that understood?'

'Yes, and may you rot in hell.'

'Two days then out; do you want try for just one day, Feltsham?'

Feltsham remained silent.

When the guardian had gone, he wrapped what belongings he had into a makeshift bag and sat on his straw bed.

The feminist movement women did protest, rotten tomatoes and apples were thrown at them, while the police watched.

'Is there no justice in England, Justin?'

'The police regard your protests as a public disturbance, Beth, using up tax payers' money to control.'

'But the cause, the suffering, their fellow citizens, where is their humanity?'

'They are grateful, Beth.'

'For what?'

'That they are not in a workhouse.'

'So we sweep the poor under the carpet of our own insecurities, is that it?'

'For the moment, yes, for there is much to be done, Beth.'

'For who? The better off, and their votes, that keep politicians in the House of Parliament or the House of Lords?'

'That includes me, my dear.'

'I know there are men of good intent, but it's taking too long, much too long.'

# CHAPTER 49

Feltsham stood outside of Islington's workhouse and considered turning right or left. Both directions looked grim, harsh, and uninviting. Turning right, more out of instinct than for any other reason, he began to walk away from the workhouse.

By late evening, Feltsham still had not found a place to shelter or sleep for the night. At a small enclosed area of ground, to his relief, he saw a wooden bench and sat down exhausted.

'What have we got here then?' a voice called out.

Looking up, Feltsham saw a black-caped policeman standing over him.

'Just sitting for a moment or so, officer. Please, I have been walking for hours and I'm exhausted.'

'I'm patrolling to the end of this street and when I come back, if you are still here, I'll charge you with vagrancy, understood?'

'Yes, I'll be gone.'

Standing, he decided to move on right away, walking in the opposite direction to the policeman. It was beginning to get dark and he desperately needed to find a place to sleep, preferably of out of sight of any passing police, but where?

Passing a bridge, he looked under the arches only to find the sleeping bodies of tramps and paupers of all descriptions. One had lit a small fire and was cooking something or other. The aroma caught in the air; it served to make him feel hungry. His last meal had been the night before in the workhouse.

Falling over a body he stretched out his hand. 'Can you spare a mouthful?'

'Fuck off before I hit you with this walking stick.'

It was now dark and getting colder by the minute. 'Dear God,' he said out loud to the growing darkness. 'Is there no end to this living nightmare?'

In the early hours of the morning, finding a residential park gate open, he collapsed onto a stone bench, having first closed the gate.

The following day he joined a queue at the dispensary relief office on St Marylebone Road. After a long wait, he was given some clothing against the cold nights and a small amount of coin called casual payments relief. Not a great deal but something, which Feltsham felt almost tearfully grateful for.

Sharing a bench with four other paupers that night, he learned about the risky life on the streets of London in 1885. 'We are no more than outcasts, my friend, doomed to roam the bitter streets of this city.'

Another recommended London Bridge to find a place to sleep. So it went on, the poor trying to help the poor, a hopeless task.

The police kept moving them on, or arresting some on the old Vagrancy Act.

'Did you find him, Beth?'

'No, I have been to every park in the area around the workhouse. Just no sign of him.'

'He may have been moved on a number of times, my dear, as a vagrant. We are in fact reviewing the Act now in the House with the intention of making it more relevant to current circumstances, but these things take time.'

'And of course there are no votes of any substance to benefit from,' Beth said.

'That's not fair. We have a large agenda to cover, Beth. You must realise that.'

'Of course, but in the meantime the poor and destitute of society go without a roof over their heads or food in their stomachs.'

'It's Lady Hastings to see you, ma'am.'

'Show her into the drawing room, Mary.'

'Florrie, this is a pleasant surprise. When did you arrive in town?'

'Late last night, but this morning, while in a hansom cab to go shopping, I'm sure I saw Feltsham, in rags it's true, and limping, but I'm sure it was him. He was turning into Regent's Park. I know you have been searching for him these past weeks. We sat looking at him all those months in the Old Bailey. I'm sure it was him.'

'Go now, Beth, before he's moved on,' Justin said.

The carriage stopped at the first entrance to the park. 'Do you want me to come with you, Lady Standish?' Robert said.

'No, we'll be fine, Robert, thank you. Just wait here.'

'I hope I'm right, Beth,' Florrie said.

'Let's go and see.'

The bench held, what appeared to Beth to be, a bag of old rags, which turned out to be Feltsham.

An eye and a half looked up at them. 'Well I must say I did not expect to see you again, Beth Shenkin, and her ladyship too. Welcome to my abode. Regrettably, it's the servant's day off so we'll have to fend for ourselves. I'd stand but I have some difficulty in that area of life.'

'Please remain sitting, Algernon. On the chance that it really was you that Lady Hastings saw, I have brought you a small chicken pie and a money belt with some florins stitched into the lining, which I hope are helpful to you.'

'I wish, ladies, that I could afford to say no to your generosity but...'

Beth cut him short, 'Perhaps I may come again to see you, Algernon, would that be possible?'

'I am mostly at home, Lady Standish. Not always on this bench for I sleep in a hideaway in the bushes opposite.'

'I understand, we'll let you get on with your meal.'

# CHAPTER 50

'The conditions for these homeless people are appalling, Justin. Something must be done. I am writing an editorial about it in our women's paper this month. Is there anything more you can do in parliament?'

'A petition may be possible. I'll look into it.'

'The writer Charles Dickens illustrates the pauper's plight so well in his novels, but to see and experience it up close as I did when going into the workhouse and again seeing Feltsham on a park bench was still a shock. His novel *Hard Times* was first published in 1854 and perfectly captures the predicament of the lower classes, but little has changed in all the years since, Justin, nothing.'

Beth met with Feltsham again. She had donated money to the workhouse to build a safe room for the babies, with a doctor to visit them every month. Her pioneering work for women's equality, the promotion of suffrage and votes for women continued over the years.

In the summer of 1889, East London was the scene of unrest as dock workers fought for better pay and working conditions. BKSS took delivery of their first all-steam-propulsion-powered ship. She was launched at Merseyside in Liverpool where Lady Hastings agreed to christen her.

In a loud clear voice, Florrie said, 'I christen this ship the *SS Shenkin*, God bless her and all who sail in her.' The champagne bottle burst on the bow and slowly she moved down the slipway into the water.

Samuel Harrison smiled from the bridge, as a fanfare played out from the brass band on the dock side. Lord Hastings turned to Beth. 'You must be very proud of what you have achieved, Beth.'

'Many made this possible, James, from a convict called Regan O'Hara to Sir Edward Standish and an Aboriginal called Tinker and many more who played their part in Shenkin's life. I am most grateful to them for it means his legacy is secure.'

The Conservative government, led by the Marquess of Salisbury, Robert Gascoyne-Cecil, asked Justin if he could send a minister to the London Shenkin Charity Foundation with the view to possibly developing similar charities across the country.

'Good of you to invite me, Lady Standish. Your Shenkin Charity Foundations here in London, South Wales and Sydney have been a great success.'

'They are my father's legacy, Minister; it is what he wanted to achieve, to be able to help others in this often hard world.'

'Indeed. Do I take it the inmates are all from the lower classes of the general public?'

'To start with, we call them our residents, not inmates.'

'My apologies, Lady Standish, residents, of course.'

'We have a surprising mix here: two former bishops defrocked for indiscretions of the moment, who then fell on very hard times, a politician and an aristocrat, but mostly paupers who had been someone at some time but fell by the wayside of life. With nowhere to live or sleep but the streets, we take them in and give them shelter.'

The minister took notes as they walked around. Tilley brought them tea and her special biscuits, as they talked. 'Tell me, Lady Standish, what does this place mean to you?'

'To me it means that from cats to kings, we all need love, the need to know that someone cares.'

'A worthy cause indeed. Incidentally, it must cost a great deal to have so many fine plants and flowers around the Centre, does it not?'

'We shall finish our tea and I'll take you to meet the person responsible for such a display of colour.'

'I would appreciate that. I'm a very keen gardener myself, Lady Standish.'

'This way then,' said Beth, when they had finished their tea.

The aroma of roses filled the air as they entered the large garden.

'Someone would like to meet you, Algernon, to complement you on your flowers and share a moment of your time.'

The former Lord Algernon Hugo Feltsham turned his face, aglow with the fresh-scented air; he had found peace at last. Beth was pleased she had helped him find it.

'Thank you, it's always good to meet a fellow gardener.'

'I'm glad to see you're content, Algernon,' Beth said. And so would Daniel Shenkin, she thought. For it's what we do for others that matters, he would always say. A small tear formed in the corner of Beth's eye.

If you say so Shenkin, so it shall be.

# HISTORICAL NOTE

In 1868 the convict transport ship *Hougoumont* arrived in Fremantle. On board were 269 convicts, the last to be sent to Western Australia. It marked the end of eighty years of penal transportation to Australia.

The late 19th century saw a vast social change in many areas. Slavery was abolished in much of Europe and the Americas. The First Industrial Revolution had taken place which reshaped economies and societies around the world. Wind-powered sailing ships were being replaced by steam, and the Suez Canal opened in 1869. Meat and wool were being produced in Australia on a large scale and shipped to ports around the world which made our character Daniel Shenkin and others like him very wealthy men.

The Second Industrial Revolution led to even higher levels of productivity, profit and prosperity, that would continue into the 20th century.

The first electronics appeared and the first functional light bulb in 1878. The century saw an era of rapidly accelerating scientific discovery in the fields of mathematics, physics, and chemistry, which laid the groundwork for technological advancement. However, the Victorian era was still notorious for the employment of children in workhouses, factories and mines. This problem was slowly being addressed by the government. Charles Dickens and other leading figures of the time were bringing it to the public's attention as early as 1860. Incredibly, it would take almost another hundred years to see the abolition of the workhouses in England and Wales.

Sir Justin Standish and Lord Feltsham spent the night at the Spaniards Inn on Hampstead Heath before their duel the following morning. The inn, named after the Spanish Ambassador to James I of England, has a most colourful background. Rumour has it that the highwayman Dick Turpin was born there, whilst his father was the landlord in the early 1700s. It was built originally as a tollgate on the Finchley boundary and commanded a full view of the road that gentry had to use to get to their homes. So, as a tavern, highwaymen were able to pick their well-heeled prey, and it became notorious for robbery and muggings. But given its romantic setting it was very popular with many poets, writers and painters of the day. It's mentioned in Dickens's *Pickwick Papers* and Bram Stokers *Dracula*, and was frequented by Byron, Keats and Joshua Reynolds.

At the same time Liberalism was becoming the pre-eminent reform movement in Europe.

The Pentonville Model Prison's 'silent system', intended to reform prisoners, did not work. It resulted in mental illnesses, depression and suicide. In the first few years of Pentonville Prison, twenty-two prisoners went mad, twenty-six had a nervous breakdown and a number killed themselves.

But the early feminist movement paved the way for the suffragettes and the 'Votes for Women' movement in 1903 for its founder Emmeline Pankhurst.

While both Daniel and Beth Shenkin are fictitious characters, they represent the pioneering spirit that helped bring about these beneficial changes in our lives. I hope I have done them the justice they deserve. I researched and then researched the research, so any errors are entirely the fault of the author.

Davey Davies May 2024

Milton Keynes UK
Ingram Content Group UK Ltd.
UKHW031124261124
3088UKWH00002B/49